THE EASTER CONFESSION

By Charles Monagan

The characters and events portrayed in this book are fictitious. Any similarity to real persons, living or dead, is coincidental and not intended by the author.

ISBN-9798657306255

Author photo by: Liss Couch-Edwards
Printed in the United States of America

For Penner Amelia

CHAPTER 1

The boy's voice grew higher and faster as he began to list his sins. It had been only a week since his last confession, but he'd spent much of it shoveling dirt onto his young soul. The priest a little wearily leaned toward the screen that separated them. Not for the first time he noted its tiny quatrefoil pattern. He bowed his head and closed his eyes.

"I also hit my sister five times and I talked back to my mother," the boy was saying. "I stole Canada Mints from the lady who comes to clean our house—Ruth—from her coat pocket."

"You don't need to name names. You went into a coat closet to steal them?" the priest asked.

"Yes, Father."

The boy was well rehearsed, and even at age 10 was familiar with the give and take in the confessional's half-light.

"Is there anything else?"

"Can you sin against a pet, Father?"

"It's possible. What did you do?"

"I hit our puppy across the nose with a rolled-up newspaper and made her cry."

"Were you training her?"

"Yes, Father. Trying to."

"That's not a sin, not exactly, but there are gentler ways of teaching a dog how to behave. Do you understand?"

"Yes, Father."

"Is that it?"

"Yes, Father."

"You will say two Our Fathers and three Hail Marys, and you

must vow never to steal, and certainly not from those less fortunate than you are. I don't want to hear that you've done it again. Now make a good and true Act of Contrition."

When the boy was finished, he made his way to the altar rail, offered up his penance in less than a minute and left through a side door. The priest slid the screen closed but then paused before opening the one on the other side of his booth. He wanted a moment before taking on the next sinner. It was April 9, 1955, Holy Saturday, the day before Easter and traditionally the busiest evening of the year for confessions. He could hear that the cavernous Church of the Immaculate Conception, this massive ocean liner of faith, was echoing with the sounds of milling penitents—the coughing and throat clearing, the shifting lines at each confessional, the low murmur of prayer, the banging of kneelers, the shuffling footsteps of those moving, rosaries in hand, among the Stations of the Cross. With great satisfaction he imagined the enormous vaulted nave, now darkening toward evening, the blazing banks of votive candles by the main altar and the distant flickering red of sub-altars in the far back corners. Most potent of all was the acrid aroma of incense that lingered from the Maundy Thursday foot washing and a funeral High Mass held earlier that day.

He gave in to the fleeting vain thought that his line might be longer than those of the other priests currently on duty. Was this because he was more understanding, he wondered, or did he just give out softer penances? Did people like him better? Was he more popular? Could he be handsomer? It was an entirely unworthy, even sinful, direction for his thoughts to travel. He brought them back, away from himself and onto some of the people, both known and unknown to him, who'd come for forgiveness. There'd been the three Burns sisters, never married, living together with their bachelor brother in the old family house, incapable of any kind of sin beyond careless gossiping. There was the stutterer who'd taken forever to confess to impure thoughts regarding a neighbor, then the college girl who'd copied test answers from another, the man with intemperate thoughts regarding Con Edison in New York, and of course the endless Saturday evening stream of swearing little boys. There was also the man who'd worn his hat into the confessional.

"I'm sorry, Father, it's been a long time," he'd said upon removing it. He spoke with a distinctively gravelly voice and a flat, toneless accent, probably Lithuanian.

"That's all right, it happens. I even did it once myself," the priest said, trying to put the man at ease.

There was a pause.

"Please begin," the priest said.

"Bless me Father for I have sinned."

Another pause. Almost invariably those words are spoken matter-of-factly, as befitting a well-worn ritual. They are delivered with the knowledge that forgiveness will very soon be granted and an open path to salvation re-established. But sometimes, very rarely, the good feeling of routine absolution isn't there at all, and the words unexpectedly become menacing and strange, as if spoken for the first time: *I have sinned.*

"When did you last make a confession?" the priest asked.

"To be honest, I can't tell you," the man said.

"That's all right. What is it that you'd like to confess?"

Another pause and then the man stumbled nervously over his words. Like the boy, he had rehearsed, too, but not as well.

"My problem is . . . what I came to you for . . . is to know in God's eyes what's a sin and what's an actual crime."

"You believe that you've committed a crime?"

"Yes, Father, without a doubt I have," the man said. "Maybe too big to forgive. Maybe too dangerous for you to even know about."

They were words that the priest hadn't heard before, and, as he later was to recall with shame, his first thought was of the long line outside the confessional and the desire to get them all out the door, into their cars and on their way home by 7 p.m. Not that they wouldn't keep the confessionals open if need be. Everyone was entitled to receive Communion on Easter Sunday—indeed it was mandatory. But this man sounded troubled, and his sin, his *crime*, seemed like it must be very real. The priest looked up to continue the conversation, to at least in some small way address his question, but the man was no longer there. He had managed to get away through the curtain without a sound, like a fish slipping the hook and returning to the anonymity of the stream.

The priest would not, could not, leave his post to pursue the man and bring him back. The people waiting patiently in line would think it unusual enough to see a man leave the confessional and not go to the communion rail—they really didn't need to see the priest come running out, too. Monsignor Shutt, the hard-knuckled senior pastor, was a believer in old-fashioned decorum in his church, and in strict order, obeisance and cleanliness in general. He would not like one of his men flapping wildly down the aisle in sight of all, not at this solemn time, not with the Lord's gruesome death so recently having been mourned.

The priest readjusted his position in the confessional. The metallic taste in his mouth, familiar from his days in the Philippines, told him that danger, alarmingly real, had visited but then moved on. He regained his composure patiently, breath by breath, and even became philosophical. A big one may have gotten away, but there were many others, smaller ones, lined up outside, waiting to be heard. Their forgiveness was just as important. He lost himself once again in their warm pool of wrongdoing and sorrow, and he let time pass. The rituals comforted and quieted. The penitents returned to their homes. As night fell, a team of volunteers came in with their carts of potted lilies and transformed the altar into an urban Easter garden with an overpowering funerary aroma. The priest and his fellows repaired to the rectory next door for a plain supper before retiring. As he drifted off to sleep, he reviewed his own status with the Lord and again found himself wanting.

◆ ◆ ◆

Easter Sunday that year in Waterbury and throughout the Northeast was exceptionally sunny and warm—hot, even—and many among the droves in church that morning, including the monsignor, gave full credit to the deity. Freed from their drab, shapeless April overcoats, the women of the city burst forth into color. After each Mass, they lingered on the Immaculate's broad front steps like finches preening on the rim of a birdbath. The daughters were resplendent, too, echoing their mothers' Easter egg purples, yellows and greens, while their brothers chafed under neckties and boxy little sports jackets. The fathers smoked in tight groups, trading small remarks and occasionally looking out for the sign to leave.

Following the 11 a.m. High Mass, the day's finale, the priest —Father Hugh Osgood—changed out of his vestments and came out into the warm sunshine. He saw that although Waterbury hadn't scheduled an Easter parade, an impromptu promenade was taking place among and between the churches that lined its central Green—two Episcopalian, one Congregational and his own. He noted that even the dour gray granite of the Protestant churches looked alive in the bright Sunday light, although nothing to match the radiant limestone of the Immaculate's Roman façade, with its welcoming "Domus Dei et Porta Coeli" etched high above the three massive front doors. If his church were located in Italy, he often thought, it would be in all the guidebooks.

But this was not the time for idle reflection—not at 1 p.m. on Easter Sunday! He hurried to the garage behind the rectory and got into his Buick coupe—black, like his rosary beads and bathing trunks. Mindful of the crowds on the sidewalks and streets, he drove slowly away from the Green, up Prospect Street, past the century-old White and Hubbard mansions and their sprawling Yankee-built neighbors. At the top of Prospect, he turned left onto Buckingham Street, and soon, with his car windows wide open, he could hear the Gill matinee, which had already spilled out of the house and onto the sunsplashed back patio.

The light of the Easter sky seemed to fall naturally upon the Gills. They were not an especially old Waterbury family, but among the many Irish Catholic upstarts, they had assimilated most successfully into the stubborn Anglo-Saxon hierarchy. Old man Oliver Gill, now long gone, had been a relentless, tireless 19th-century entrepreneur, with an active hand or two in local coal, oil, ice and lumber enterprises, and even a little banking and lawmaking, too. With his passing in 1935, his five children were already comfortably arrayed across the city's hills. The youngest, today's host, Peter, had become a distinguished member of the medical profession, a pediatrician with five children of his own. The Gill scorecard showed not a bolter, not a black sheep, across three generations—not unless you wanted to count Doc Gill's oldest son, Dan, the priest's best friend, who had tossed all respectability aside to become a newspaper reporter.

It was Danny who was loitering alone by the side gate, smoking, when Father Osgood arrived, bearing a large display of lilies.

"You've been cast out," the priest said to his old friend. "And on Easter of all days. Has someone finally taken offense?"

"Offense to what, possibly?" Danny asked with a grin, flicking an ash onto a stone step.

"Just general, I suppose. On principal."

"My mother doesn't like smokers near the food."

His mother was a Goodyear from Buffalo. She was kind-hearted and good, yet somehow always got her way.

"She'd have a tough time in the rectory," said Father Osgood. "The dining room is usually choking in a Chesterfield haze.

"I didn't think you needed food, living on prayer as you do," said Danny. "Speaking of which, Happy Easter! How did it go?"

"Record numbers. Four of us on the rail."

Danny stubbed out his smoke and flicked the butt up onto the street.

"You look good, Dan," Father Osgood said. "You've got some color for a change."

"It's a story I'm working on."

The priest looked at him expectantly.

"An art theft," Dan said with a touch of confidentiality. "A big one. But I don't want to say too much more about it right now.

My deadline looms. What you're seeing in my cheeks is the flush of panic."

The priest thought he could count on two hands, maybe two fingers, the number of Waterbury families that owned "big" art collections.

"It sounds very wartime France," he said.

"You'd be surprised," said Danny. "C'mon, let's go see who's here."

They strolled around the side of the house to the rear, where the planned indoor buffet had spontaneously been moved out onto a flagstone patio and expansive grassy surround. Gills of all ages and sizes were gathered, talking animatedly, even laughing and shouting, in the unprecedented warm light. A few close friends and neighbors had gained admission as well. The priest always felt an extra measure of affection on days like this, holy days, and he reveled in it as he rounded the corner.

"Here he is, the man of the hour!" Dr. Gill shouted, raising the first gin and tonic of the season in the priest's direction.

Father Osgood pointed a cautionary finger toward the heavens.

"Not quite," he said to general laughter, for now all eyes were upon him.

One of the grandchildren made a ceremonial path from the bar with a Cutty Sark and water in hand. The long Lenten drought could now be broken.

"Bless you, child," he said, again to laughter, as he took the glass. "Take these lilies to your grandma, please." He was with friends—family, practically—so he could joke and loosen his collar a bit. He sipped the amber as the others turned back to their own conversations.

In 1955, it was not at all uncommon for well-to-do Catholic families to informally adopt a priest—he was always welcome for Sunday dinner, to listen to or watch a game, for birthdays and other special occasions. There was a designated armchair for him to sit in, an ashtray, a drink. All offers of help, to do the dishes or mash the potatoes, were rejected out of hand, although a small gift such as a spray of flowers or a tin of English toffees was always welcome. Occasionally an invitation to Yale Bowl or a symphony concert could be extended. And of course being present at Easter dinner was as obligatory for the priest as attendance at Easter Mass was for his congregants.

Such was the case with Father Osgood and the Gills, but with a major difference. They had known him since he was a boy from the neighborhood and best friends with their own Danny. He'd historically been seen by Dan's parents as a good influence on their son—polite, a hard worker, a mature decision maker. He'd always been a welcome presence in their house, especially after his own doting parents—Hugh was an only child—had been killed by a drunken driver when he was 16 and he'd fallen under the nervous guardianship of a maiden aunt. A few years later, Hugh became even more welcome when he unexpectedly declared himself for the priesthood. Mrs. Gill might have regretted losing Hugh as a possible match for one of her daughters, but a calling was a calling and there was no use fighting it.

Danny saw Hugh in a somewhat different light. Hugh had given him his first cigarette, a Sweet Caporal swiped from his father's cardigan pocket in 1935. He'd also produced a memorably warm and revolting quart of beer two years later, when they were 12. And he always seemed to have firecrackers on hand, obtained from a secret source. Over the years they'd been through a lot together, first at Driggs, the neighborhood grammar school, with its impressive melting-pot mix of students and core of no-nonsense, Normal School-trained teachers. Next came four years together at the city's Crosby High School, the ivy-walled college-track institution where scholarship was revered, along with football, and Latin could still be heard spoken in the hallways. The war sent them off singly to distant corners of the world and eventually steered them into far different callings. But here they were now, back in Waterbury where they began, best friends once again.

Hugh savored the slight disorientation brought on by the Cutty Sark and took a moment to observe the scene before him.

The Gills and their guests were now lining up at the impromptu outdoor buffet table, which was laden with a ham, a leg of lamb, deep dishes of scalloped potatoes, green beans amandine, and crusty crescent hard rolls. He relished the feeling of the sun on the back of his neck and felt lucky. This was the life he'd longed for while he was in the Pacific. Not simple-minded, but safe and predictable, with ordinary pleasures. Dan was different in that respect, a little less easily satisfied. His war, less bloody than Hugh's, hadn't much curbed his youthful appetite for risk and danger, nor for righting wrongs. Unlike Hugh, he'd still walk through—would relish walking through—the unmarked doorway. Hugh now looked around for him, but saw that he'd slipped away, no doubt with a tenderly prepared picnic basket to enjoy as he worked on his story.

Eventually, everyone loaded up a plate and found a place to sit. Doctor Gill stood and offered a toast to the day and the shared delight in having such a family and friends. He then called upon Hugh to say grace, which he did easily and freely, the words flowing prettily but not for too long. It was only a minute or two after he finished the blessing that a bank of clouds sped across the sun and a breeze picked up, the first indication of a predicted cool front moving in from the west. The rain didn't begin until later, after the guests had left and the well-orchestrated cleanup returned the yard and patio to their original condition. Hugh drove back to the rectory, enjoyed a quick cigarette alone in the parlor, and then made his way up to his room, where he found he had to close his window against the sudden damp and chill. Easter Sunday was at last at an end, but the rain continued on, eventually pounding on the rectory's sturdy roof, the forerunner of the wettest spring and summer that anyone could remember.

CHAPTER 2

Danny Gill's story broke on Tuesday. It was positioned on the front page in a way—huge and bold—to take the city by storm. "BIG ART THEFT," the headline blared. Beneath it, a secondary deck read, "$300K in Paintings Taken From Wheeler Estate," and then one line below: "Chauffeur Missing." The story itself revealed that four paintings by the French artists Monet, Manet and Degas had apparently been stolen during the week leading up to Easter from the Wheeler mansion on Hillside Avenue. The Wheelers, a major force in Waterbury's industrial epoch and widely considered to be the city's wealthiest family, had been away on a holiday trip to Bermuda, leaving "Morningside," their prominent Queen Anne style house, in the hands of two housemaids and their chauffeur/gardener, Thomas Murphy, who seemed to have disappeared during the period in question.

"These are valuable artworks," the chief of police was quoted as saying, mustering as much authority as he could regarding French paintings. "They'll be very hard for a common thief to unload if that's the intention," he continued. "I don't think they'll get far. Our first order of business is to find this Thomas Murphy and bring him in for questioning."

The article went on to explain that the paintings had for more than 50 years been displayed on the walls of Morningside. They represented only a small portion of the Wheelers' overall collection but were by far the most valuable, according to Dr. Anibel Moss, the director of the local Mattatuck Museum and holder of an advanced degree in Art History.

"Whoever took these paintings knew what they were

doing," she said. "The works by the Impressionists are gaining in value every week, it seems."

It was she who placed the total value of the heist at around $300,000.

Father Osgood read the story at the breakfast table after celebrating the 7 a.m. Mass. The daybreak service, performed at its customary lightning speed, had been attended by several dozen daily communicants along with a few less familiar early risers. Everyone had come to the rail. Now, with his stomach rumbling and the taste of wafer and wine lingering on his tongue, he looked forward to Mrs. Dunn's Tuesday special: silver dollar pancakes drenched with warm syrup accompanied by a pot of strong rectory coffee.

Danny's story was a meal in itself, with quotes from at least 20 people, a take on the Wheelers, their estate and the source of their wealth, background color on the art world in general and a recap of notable recent thefts. He even included a quote from an expert at the FBI laying out what might happen next.

"The rank amateur would try to sell them on the street, or possibly hold them for ransom," he said. "Someone more connected would try to sell them into the international black market, or maybe already had a buyer. Or it could be that the thief will simply hold onto the paintings and not make a move right away. Maybe they're already hanging in someone's den. Or maybe they're out of their frames, rolled up and stored in a vault or a barn loft someplace. There are a lot of ways this can go."

When he was done reading, Hugh noted with a thin smile that Dan yet again had gone to Anibel for a quote. Given her knowledge of the art world, as well as the principals involved, her inclusion was well justified, he thought. Maybe Dan's longtime devotion to Anibel, largely unrequited, hadn't factored into his choice of her as a source for the story. Still, Hugh was amused by how many times Anibel had appeared in Dan's reporting over the years. It was pretty clear that it was his way, or one of them, of keeping the old flame burning.

Those personal factors aside, though, it was a terrific local story. Hugh could see why Danny had been so nervous about its scope and accuracy. Not only that, but it would doubtless be a continuing story, with frequent updates and new developments. He couldn't wait to congratulate his friend and playfully quiz him about his actual knowledge of the painters in question.

◆ ◆ ◆

The first new development was an enormous one, and it came just a couple of days later. Again under Daniel Gill's byline, the story announced that the body of Thomas Murphy, the erstwhile chauffeur/gardener and presumably the prime suspect, had been found dumped alongside an out-of-the-way bend in the rain-swollen Naugatuck River. He'd been tied up hand and foot, shot three times in the neck and head and wrapped in a Tabriz rug that had been taken from Morningside's entry hall. The art theft, it now appeared, had been complicated by murder.

Hugh soaked in all the details but concluded that because of the man's death the story had moved beyond his ability to openly enjoy. It had entered a darker realm. Anyone, even a priest, could appreciate a well-crafted art theft—the planning, daring and stealth often made for an irresistible tale, one that was easy to romanticize. The team of burglars, the moonless night, the dark museum or mansion, the perfect strategy with all the pieces falling into place—it was hard not to root on some level for the effort and cunning involved. But now a possibly innocent man's life had been taken. Whether he'd been part of the theft or merely an unlucky bystander didn't matter, at least not to Hugh. Any notion of romance in the story had been snuffed. The thieves had gone too far. He'd continue reading about the case, of course, and still looked forward to talking to Danny about it. But the illicit thrill could no longer be there for him.

Or so he thought. By chance, Hugh and Dan bumped into each other that evening. Hugh was looking in briefly on the women's Holy Name Society meeting in his church's cavernous basement hall, when Dan came in to drop his mother off at the same get-together. As the women prepared to discuss their possible supportive role in the missionary effort to bring relief to the war-torn Korean Peninsula, Hugh congratulated Dan on his big scoop.

"You really covered all the bases, Dan," he said. "I haven't seen a story like that in the local rag in years."

"Always nice to get a pat on the back, Hugh. Thanks."

"The latest complication is a horror, though."

"Yeah, the body is making the cops close ranks on things a bit."

"What do you mean?"

"I'm trying to do some digging on exactly how the chauffeur's death, or just the chauffeur himself, might tie in with the theft and they're getting awfully tight-lipped."

"Well, they probably don't know themselves."

"Maybe not. All they say to me unofficially is that the whole thing smells like an out-of-town job."

"Meaning?"

Despite his earlier resolve, Hugh was caving in to a deepening interest in the story.

"They won't say," answered Dan. "Maybe they think it was too professional for the local criminal class? Maybe guys here are too lowbrow to have much of an interest in valuable art or a clue about how to fence paintings?"

"Well, it doesn't seem very professional to me," Hugh said.

Dan smiled.

"First of all, someone was murdered," Hugh continued. "That shouldn't have to happen in the course of a common art theft, should it?"

"How much do you know about art thefts?"

"Enough," said Hugh.

"Well, you're probably right, but maybe Murphy's job was just to get the thieves into the house. Once he did that, they didn't need him anymore," Dan said.

"So they killed him? That seems drastic."

"Well then, maybe he tried to change the deal he had, to increase his payoff, and threatened to talk if he didn't get it."

"Or?" Hugh hung the word out like bait.

There was a pause. The women were calling their meeting to order.

"Okay," Danny said. "Or what?"

"Or maybe the thieves *were* all local guys and they knew one another, and they decided they couldn't risk being identified by Murphy, who was a known entity associated with the house and would certainly be brought in for questioning. Maybe they didn't trust that paying him off would be enough to prevent him from getting scared and talking."

Dan now studied his friend, marveling at his level of interest.

"I think the boys at police headquarters might be interested in your various theories," he said.

Hugh smiled sheepishly and looked over to where the women were beginning to settle in.

"Anyway," he said in a near whisper. "I'm actually a little worried about the theft side of the story."

"What about it?"

"I wonder if it's a one-time deal or should we be worried about more? We've got some valuable things—gold mostly, even solid gold—upstairs."

Danny shrugged.

"Who knows?" he said. "I have a feeling there's going to be more news every day on this."

"And it's your story."

"Yes, it's all mine for now, although I've heard the *Times* is sending someone up, and some of these television news guys are getting pretty professional. Oh, and by the way, Hugh," Dan continued, his voice growing confidential, "you'll be interested to know I got my first death threat yesterday."

"You're kidding!"

"No. Someone called the newspaper's switchboard and warned that I needed to watch my step or else. A male voice. The poor switchboard operator was beside herself. I think she took the rest of the day off."

"Do you think it was serious?"

"Who knows? It doesn't seem like something a seasoned professional art thief would do. More likely, it was a crank call. I think I'm supposed to wear it as a badge of honor. Anyway, that's all I know for now. I've got to get back to the shop."

Hugh turned to leave as well.

"Say hi to your Mom for me, Dan," he said. "And be careful!"

Dan nodded and raced out the basement's side door.

One thing Hugh Osgood liked to do to break up the routines of his day in the church and rectory was to walk over to the central post office on Grand Street and pick up the day's mail for the parish. The walk was a short one, only about 10 minutes, but it took him back and forth through the heart of what was, by all appearances, a thriving, well-ordered New England industrial city—for more than 100 years one of the nation's most progressive and prosperous cities. Indeed, Hugh thought that Waterbury's story could serve as a chapter in America's larger tale: how, after a long, dangerous, dirty, disease-ridden, often God-damned start based on trying to farm the thin valley soil, the English settlers didn't quit or move away—they rolled up their sleeves and began making things. First came a trickle of buttons, then a steadier stream of items like shelf clocks and kettles, and finally a raging torrent of hundreds of manufactured products, especially those made from brass. It was Waterbury's factory-produced brass—pipes, wire and tubing, rivets, belt buckles, subway tokens and much, much more—that had created jobs and decent livings for thousands of newcomers from all over the world, and vast fortunes for those at the top of the heap.

Hugh saw the evidence of this affluence every day as he made his walk for the mail. Here were the imposing central churches, including his own, built with donations great and small, and the downtown banks with their grand, confident facades. Rising up to the west was the astonishing Italianate train tower, an apparent tribute to a similar tower in Siena, the Tuscan hill town. Grand Street was home to a harmonious cluster of commercial and government buildings, including the post office itself, a marble-clad Art Deco gem with expert exterior carvings tracing the history of transportation from horseback to the airliner. Taken as a whole, Hugh often thought as he made his rounds, it was all the grandeur that the brass money could commission and pay for—even if, as some now whispered, the air was at last beginning to escape the city's long economic balloon ride. And, of course, sprinkled among the downtown treasures were the lower-profile essentials, the diners and clothing shops, the dry cleaners, record shops, pool halls and package stores. And always the stream of people moving among them—at work, on errands or idle, devout or profane, well off or barely getting by. Hugh saw them all and felt a sense of belonging and even custodianship, not only for the ones who were his parishioners, but for all of them. In the city's busy daily choreography, everyone had a role to play.

On this day, Hugh was lamenting to himself the sudden intrusion of theft and murder into what was normally a peaceable stroll when he'd gotten further sidetracked onto the nature of the stolen paintings themselves. He was a little familiar with the French Impressionists. He knew about Monet and his haystacks. He wondered about the artist's urge to paint the same subject over and over again. Degas with his many depictions of ballerinas was another one. He then strayed further to thoughts about his own trip to Paris some years earlier and his sudden obsessive need to return to Notre Dame Cathedral every day he was there. All the rest of Paris beckoned seductively, including its art museums and galleries, but instead he found himself back at the Isle de la Cite, gazing up at the formidable Medieval twin towers like someone under hypnosis, and then again and again climbing up to the top to feel and smell in the stone and timbers the far, unknowable reaches of faith. Had his repeated daily climb been in the same league as the painters' artistic obsessions? Possibly, but he never had a chance to address that one. Instead, he got pulled back to Waterbury with a worldly thump.

"Hey, Father!"

"Good morning," Hugh said automatically.

"The sun feels good."

"Yes, it does."

He was halfway up Leavenworth Street. The voice had come from the top of an alley next to Jimmy's Heel Bar, a shoe-shine and shoe-repair shop. Now the man stepped out onto the sidewalk. He was a familiar Waterbury type, short and squat with a high Eastern European forehead, blonde hair combed straight back. He wore an open-necked short-sleeve shirt that emphasized his powerful upper body. He could probably throw a good punch, and take one, too. Hugh smiled genially as he tried to place the voice, which he felt he knew.

"You're Father Osgood from the Immaculate," the man said.

"Yes, that's right."

Now Hugh knew the voice. It was the one from the confessional the other day, the one that got away. The sweet morning air was suddenly charged with uncertainty. Hugh thought he might still get away with a look at his watch and quick nod, but the man stepped directly into his path.

"That's a beautiful church," he said.

"Yes, it is."

"We met the other day, you know."

"Yeah, you're the one who skipped out on me."

Could he say that much? He wasn't sure. It was certainly customary not to acknowledge those who'd been to him for confession. Over the years, he'd recognized many voices of friends and acquaintances—some of them with surprising stories to tell—without ever revealing a word of it. But this man hadn't actually confessed to anything. He hadn't gotten that far.

"I got cold feet," he said.

"It happens," said Hugh.

"I was embarrassed."

"No need."

"Ashamed."

Hugh made another polite move to get by.

"You weren't the only one I confessed to, Father," the man continued.

"You didn't actually confess, if you recall."

"Yeah, but you can probably put two and two together."

"What do you mean?"

"I'm sure you saw the newspaper."

Could he mean the art theft? The murder? Hugh was now being carried out into uncharted waters.

"You're probably thinking I was one of the ones who took the paintings, but that's not it," the man continued. He was just blurting out stuff now, and rather loudly, too. Hugh looked around to see if anyone could have overheard. Inside the shoe bar, Sandy Jones sat up high, getting the daily shine applied to his custom-made two-tones. Across the street, Hoddy Franklin rushed in through his bank's side door with a fresh box of cigars under his arm. Others walked by on both sides of the street, but it appeared that no one had heard anything.

"Look," he said to the man, "this is not a confessional and this is not a confession. I will hear your confession if you wish, either in the rectory or in church, but now is not the time and Leavenworth Street is definitely not the place. What you really need to do right now is go to the police."

With that, the man backed off.

"Not gonna do that," he said. "Can't do that at all."

He looked around as he spoke, as if for the first time realizing he wasn't being careful and that he needed to be. He wiped his perspiring forehead with a handkerchief.

"I'll come to the rectory," he continued. "When would be a good time for that?"

"I'm usually there. You can come with me right now if you want."

"Thanks, but no, Father. I've got a few things to take care of first. Maybe this afternoon."

The men parted at last. As he made his way to the post office and then back home again, Hugh's heart raced. Had he overstepped his bounds? He honestly couldn't say. The man had been desperate for help, both in the confessional and now out on the street. Had Hugh let him down? What more could he have done—literally drag him into the confessional? In any case, all he could do now was wait for the man's knock on the rectory door. But the knock never came. Instead, two days later he opened up the morning paper to see the man's face staring back at him with the accompanying news that Theodore Valuckas, husband and father of two, was suddenly no more, dead of what the paper termed "natural causes" at the age of 39.

CHAPTER 3

Burdened with unasked-for, unwanted knowledge involving what appeared to be criminal wrongdoing, Hugh was uncertain about where to turn. He couldn't go to the police because he felt that Valuckas' words to him could be construed in some small sense as a confession and thus were required by Church rules to be kept secret. He couldn't go to the Catholic hierarchy because he didn't want to become the pawn in a painful game of situation ethics, full of pronouncements, pipe smoking and accusatory frowns, ending six months later with very little clarity or understanding and definitely erring on the side of self-preservation for the Church. He couldn't go to Dan and the newspaper because he had no desire to be an active source in a story of theft and, it now seemed very possible, multiple murders. But what was he to do? He suddenly seemed to be right at the center of a huge, violent story—at ground zero, to use the newly popular term. He likely possessed knowledge no one else had, or almost no one. The thieves and their treasure might be getting further and further away or burrowing deeper into hiding. But something told him they weren't going anywhere—they were local guys, or why else would a mug like Valuckas be involved? Because of that, he thought he might be able to move with deliberation. There wouldn't be any sudden, rash moves from him. Instead, he'd get started on some homework. Which is why a few days after the Valuckas obit, he found himself walking across the Green for a meeting of his own with Dr. Anibel Moss.

He might not have gone to Anibel had it not been for her authoritative presence in Dan's initial article. They hadn't spoken in quite some time, not since a late winter dinner party when the hosts had innocently seated them next to each other and he once again felt himself falling helplessly into orbit around her. The two of them, along with Dan, made for a complicated story now more than a decade in the making. She'd been another member of their high school class at Crosby, where she'd arrived at the beginning of junior year as a dazzling "new girl," sending ripples across the school's otherwise placid social pond. She'd come up from Georgia with her family, her father having taken a job at one of the brass companies' headquarters. She was an exotic addition to the day-to-day at Crosby, an intriguing, sweetly accented Southern girl, brilliant in all her classes and very different from the hometown girls in her manner, outlook and appearance. She didn't appeal to every boy, but she certainly appealed to Hugh and Dan.

The other kids in high school—sometimes facetiously, sometimes not—called Hugh and Dan "Cooper and Flynn," as if they were a team, which in a way, as the closest of friends, they were. Hugh had Gary Cooper's bright eyes and laconic manner. He was smart and dependable and knew when to be quiet, and the loss of his parents drew an attractive aura of tragedy around him wherever he went. Dan, on the other hand, was from far more affluent and less tragic circumstances. He was a fast, bright, blond-haired seducer, and strikingly handsome in an Errol Flynn sort of way. His smile was widely seen as charming, with a life of its own, but also quite possibly signaling trouble somewhere up the road. Yes, they were best friends, but that never kept them from competing for girls. Indeed, they often enjoyed the competition—at least until the new girl came along.

Hugh got there first with Anibel. In mid-September, the school year having barely begun, their English teacher had the two of them read aloud a passage from "Our Town," the one in which George Gibbs and Emily Webb sit together at a drug store counter and fall in love over strawberry ice cream sodas. It was a supercharged passage to read in front of the whole class, and Hugh always suspected the teacher, Mr. Reardon, of slyly playing the matchmaker. In any case, it worked. He never forgot the tingle he felt as he read his lines and Anibel read alongside him, her soft cadences full of youthful longing—actual longing, he thought, that he could perhaps redirect toward him. So he asked her out, and, with Dan on the sidelines openly regretting his third-wheel status, they quickly became an item. Of course, she turned out to be nothing like Emily Webb. Anibel Moss was a college-bound, modern girl with ambitions that carried well beyond hopes for marriage and children and simple homespun pleasures. Hugh at the time liked to think of himself as one of the big men on campus, a real Waterbury sophisticate, but Anibel knew how to tease him with her superior knowledge of world and cultural events, and with her libertine Protestant ideas. Her talk of Picasso and Karl Marx made Hugh realize just how sheltered he'd been. As to sex, they were powerfully attracted to one another but technically remained chaste, even after multiple opportunities. As it turned out, Hugh was still a little careful and old-fashioned —maybe even fearful—when it came to sexual maneuvering. He never was brave enough to voice his misgivings outright, but he always found a reason to step back before plunging into the depths of a full, freefalling, carnal relationship. Anibel went along with it, thinking she could bring him along gradually. They both thought everything might change—would certainly change —once they got to college.

But it being June 1943 when they graduated, the world demanded its toll. Shortly after their commencement ceremonies, and following difficult conversations at home, Hugh and Dan drove downtown together and signed up to fight in the war. Suddenly no plan was safe. The boys were to be away for a long while, on opposite sides of the globe, while Anibel went off to Smith College in Massachusetts. There was a tacit understanding that she would be there for Hugh when he returned, but when the war ended and he finally did get back to the States, he'd been stood on his head and could think only of becoming a priest. Anibel took this as a terrible blow, in many ways unfathomable, but Dan took it as an opportunity. After a suitable period had passed, he approached her with an offer of what he called "a special friendship." To him, this meant they could acknowledge the loss of her romance with Hugh while still embracing each other. He made known his longtime affection for her and tried to convince her that she could still be happy with him. But it was a move from one best friend to another that she just couldn't make. Her heart remained with Hugh. Dan, although she loved him, too, and even allowed him some intimacy, just seemed like an impossible leap, like going from brother to brother.

In the years that followed the war, they each took separate paths away from Waterbury and then back again. Hugh entered the seminary, was ordained five years later, served as an assistant pastor in Baltimore for two years and then found himself assigned to the Immaculate Conception, the church in which he'd been confirmed. Dan went to Fordham and then on to a small daily paper in Rhode Island, where, helped by his wartime experience with *Stars and Stripes*, he moved quickly up through the ranks. After a couple of years, the tug of his family ties brought him back to Waterbury. As for Anibel, her many successes at Smith took her to a doctorate in Art History at NYU. While in New York, she met, briefly dated and then married a fellow student, a Yalie whose deteriorating eyesight had kept him out of combat, and soon—as he faced the impossible prospect of being the world's first blind Art History expert—turned him to drink. The marriage lasted only a little longer than the dating had, and Anibel, her pride deeply wounded, retreated back home to her parents. What was meant to be a brief respite in Waterbury turned, with the luck of good timing and a few connections, into the top job at the museum at a remarkably young age.

◆ ◆ ◆

So, yes, a complicated set of relationships, and very much on Hugh's mind as he made his way up the museum's front steps and through a maze of construction sawhorses to Anibel's office. She was perched on an assistant's desk, chatting, as he approached. She glanced up at him, then quickly away, and then stood, smiling, to greet him. Hugh was pleased to see she remained every inch a Smithie. Her soft, brownish-red shoulder-length hair was parted to one side and held in place with a barrette. Her calf-length skirt swayed as she moved toward him. Her light wool top was pinched just a little at the waist. Hugh tried to tell himself he'd be just as observant no matter whom he was greeting, but of course that wasn't true.

"Hugh, how are you?" she said brightly, extending a hand. Ten years had had no effect on her Georgia drawl. "Girls, this is Father Osgood from the Immaculate Conception across the Green. He and I are members of the greatest class in the history of Crosby High."

Hugh smiled and nodded shyly and then followed Anibel into her office.

"I'm just fine, Anibel, and happy to see you again," he said a little stiffly, "although I almost took a wrong turn into your construction project downstairs."

"Sorry about that," she said. "We're 50 years late, but we're finally beginning our transformation into the twentieth century. We're storing away the old artifacts and bringing in art and history pieces that actually have something to do with our part of the world."

"Won't the donors be upset?"

"You mean the globe-trotters who never forgot to bring us back little souvenirs from their travels? They might be miffed if they were still alive, but, alas, they're long gone. Meanwhile, can I interest you in a vial containing sand from the nose of the Sphinx?"

Hugh laughed as he took a seat.

"We have more than our share of souvenirs over at our place," he said. "In fact, a couple of weeks ago someone came by and wondered if we'd be interested in purchasing a piece of the True Cross."

"How much?"

"Cross or money?"

"Money."

"I don't think we got that far."

A natural pause came in the social small talk. Hugh was never one for filling conversational gaps. Instead, he was recalling with embarrassment how at the recent dinner party he'd placed a hand on Anibel's shoulder as he spoke to her and that it had felt a lot like open affection. She may have felt the same way. Now she was tilting her head in a manner that indicated he ought to get to his point in coming to see her.

"I find myself in the strangest situation, Anibel," he said.

"So you mentioned on the phone. What's it about?"

"Somehow I've gotten myself tied into the Wheeler art theft story."

Anibel looked alarmed.

"How did you do *that*?"

"Well, I possess knowledge that may be important."

"Knowledge about what?"

"I can't tell you."

"No, of course not."

Anibel got up and closed the office door. Through the big windows behind her desk, Hugh could see the stone-steepled Episcopalian church and the Civil War soldiers' monument rimming the western end of the Green.

"That's the trouble with your cult," she said, employing the word she often used when referring to his Roman faith. "You're way too wrapped up in secrecy."

Hugh could smile at her words. They weren't meant to harm, only to tease, although she'd once, long ago, tearfully and angrily told him he'd been taken away from her by a band of men dressed in robes and hoods.

"Maybe I can figure out a way to share it with you, Anibel, but not today. Today I'd love you to tell me again the story of how the Wheelers acquired their paintings in the first place."

Anibel sat back in her chair. Hugh knew it was one of her favorite topics, and something she planned to write about at length someday. He doubted she could be brief, but he didn't mind. In order to decide his next move, if there was to be one, he needed context. He felt he had to immerse himself in the whole story.

"The Wheelers of Waterbury and the Lords from Dayton were both very wealthy industrial families," she began. "They became friendly, first through shared business interests and then socially, to the extent that in 1888 they decided to take their extended families on a grand tour of Europe together."

She then in great and colorful detail told the story of that trip, and especially the way Impressionist art played a key role in it. Charles Lord and Burton Wheeler, although from different generations, were similarly passionate about finding and collecting art. With American painter Mary Cassatt as their guide, they stormed the galleries and ateliers of Paris, snapping up dozens of paintings along the way. Wheeler, only in his mid-20s and by far the younger of the two men, used the nearly limitless checkbook of his father, C.C. Wheeler, to buy what he wanted, although at what by current standards were bargain-basement prices. He showed a special liking for Monet, Degas, Whistler and Cassatt herself. As a result, the walls of the family's Waterbury mansion soon featured a Monet haystack or two, a Degas ballet rehearsal and even Whistler's notorious "Girl in White," among many others.

"They've bought, sold and traded more than a thousand pieces over the years," Anibel went on, "so it's hard to know what they've still got. The ones that were stolen were probably the cream of the collection and the ones they liked most."

"And the most valuable?"

"I'd say so."

"Worth enough to kill for?"

"Oh, yes, absolutely. I'd kill for one of the Monets alone."

Hugh smiled again. He knew Anibel could have gone into greater detail on any number of side stories—the tale of the unrequited love involving Burton Wheeler and young Josephine Lord, Mary Cassatt's coming to Waterbury to paint three Wheeler family portraits, and even, somehow in the midst of everything else, the sinking of the *Lusitania*—but she probably needed a glass of wine to do complete justice to it all. For now, this was refresher enough.

"You were called up to the house, Anibel," he said.

"Seth and Alice Wheeler wanted me to come up and help out in the aftermath of the theft. They thought I could help impress upon the police the importance of what they'd lost and a sense of urgency in getting it back."

"What do you make of it all?"

"The thieves knew what they were after, so they got good direction from someone," she said. "I know for certain that Alice Wheeler possesses a fortune in jewelry—inadequately protected, just as the paintings were—but none of it was taken. Two Monets, a Degas and a Manet—it was an art theft, pure and simple. But there is one thing, something just mentioned in passing in Danny's stories, that intrigues me."

"What's that?"

"The painting that wasn't taken."

"What do you mean?"

"There was one painting, an important Whistler, right there among the others, that was apparently never touched."

Hugh looked at her blankly.

"It's called 'Thames Nocturne,' stunning, worth plenty, sitting on the library wall right in between the two Monets," Anibel continued. "Why would they just leave it there? It doesn't make any sense to me."

"Maybe they thought they heard someone coming," Hugh offered.

"No one was coming, Hugh. The chauffeur was in on the job."

"How do you know that?"

"I'm just assuming. According to Dan's story, there was no forced entry. The family and other staff were conveniently away. Who else could be sure of that?"

She looked at Hugh closely.

"By the way, your interest in this case is unbecoming of your profession," she said.

Hugh realized he was now leaning forward in his chair, with one of his elbows actually planted on the edge of Anibel's desk.

"I know, it's awful," he said, sitting back again. He'd been trying to picture Valuckas in the scene but couldn't quite get him there. "I guess I can tell you that I have a name the police might want to consider, but because of the way I got it, I don't think I can reveal it."

"And you are the very soul of discretion."

"It goes well beyond that, as I'm sure you know."

"The seal of the confessional?"

Hugh was surprised she knew the term.

"Yes, actually."

"The secrets you must harbor. I'd never be able to do that."

"The secrets go right through me," Hugh said. "At least that's the theory."

"But not so easy in this case."

"Not so far, no."

He loved the give-and-take with Anibel, and the life in her eyes. He wondered how she, with all her gifts, could still be alone.

"Time for me to go," he said abruptly, looking at his watch and interrupting his own straying thoughts. "Past time, in fact. Thanks for all the background."

Anibel rose with him.

"Seriously, Hugh," she said, "if you need to work this out or work your way through it, let me help. I'm fascinated by it."

"By my dilemma?"

"By the case, the theft, the murder."

"Maybe we can do that," Hugh said, opening the door to leave, "and maybe bring Danny in, too." He stepped beneath the threshold and then stuck his head in again. "And may God grant that it's only one murder," he said.

Which instantly raised the stakes, and Anibel's curiosity, and all but assured that he and she would soon meet again and that the case and its many facets had now become, in some sense, a team project.

◆ ◆ ◆

After dinner that night, Hugh repaired to the rectory's library to refresh his understanding of the rules that applied to his current situation. The laws of what Anibel had called "the seal of the confessional" had repeatedly been drilled into him at the seminary. There, he'd learned that the rite of confession itself went back to the very earliest days of the Church, in fact to Jesus himself when he breathed the Holy Spirit into the apostles and told them, "Whose sins you shall forgive, they are forgiven them." Around the 7th century, the church began to organize itself with specific penances for certain sins, and then 500 years more brought the innovation of individual confessions. Still another 500 years brought the establishment of confessionals as a necessary part of church design.

Rain once again beat at the outer walls of the rectory as Hugh paged through various texts. The library, with its wood paneling and big fireplace, served as a retreat and study room of sorts for the parish's five priests. Here, they could find a decent selection of Church- and liturgy-related books and other materials, inspirational biographies and approved histories, as well as copies of *The Catholic Transcript* and *Life*, *Look* and *Time* magazines, where the fodder for Sunday sermons lay thick. From the small collection devoted to confession, Hugh pulled a familiar pamphlet dating from the early 1930s and went straight to the marvelous compilation of sins considered "grave violations of God's law that turn men away from God." What an illicit charge it must have given the committee assigned to weighing and then composing the list: *murder, idolatry, sorcery/magic, avarice, theft, jealousy, greed, hatred, love of vain glory, false witness, perjury, hypocrisy, slander, spite, anger, rebellion, argument, perverseness, bad temper, gossiping, insults, injustice, deceitfulness, pride, boastfulness, vanity, arrogance, fickleness/insanity, drunkenness and intemperance, impurity, adultery, homosexuality, fornication, pederasty, con-*

cupiscence, impure language and use of pornographic materials. The list was as long as the human story, Hugh thought. Maybe it *was* the human story. But it wasn't really what he was looking for at the moment. For that, he had to dig a little deeper into the library shelves. But there really was no need. He knew exactly, almost by heart, what he would find there.

"The sacramental seal is inviolable; therefore, it is absolutely forbidden for a confessor to betray *in any way* a penitent in words or in any manner and for any reason," one authoritative text read. "In a criminal matter, a priest may encourage the penitent to surrender to authorities, but that's the extent of the power he wields. He cannot make this a condition of the absolution *or indirectly disclose the matter to civil authorities himself.*"

But what if the penitent never actually, fully confessed? Hugh asked himself, leaning back in his chair and staring up at the library's high ceiling.

And what if he's dead?

There was no answer in the library for those questions, and indeed the Church was not very eager in general to address "what ifs?" It was much better at making saints out of priests who chose to die rather than reveal the secrets of the confessional. Hugh read some of their stories. Going way back, there was John of Nepomuk, outfitted in a suit of armor and thrown into the Moldau River in 1383 by Bohemia's King Wenceslaus when he wouldn't tell the king what the queen had said during confession. More recently, there was Matteo Correa Magallanes, a Mexican who heard the sins of Catholic revolutionaries in 1927 but refused to pass the information along to the generals. He was shot in the head while standing next to his own open grave. As recently as 1936, Fernando Olmedo Reguera was caught in a similar situation during the Spanish Civil War and was executed for his stubborn silence.

Compared to these stalwarts, Hugh thought himself insignificant. Yet he was certain that he felt the same enormous responsibility they must have known when hearing someone confess. The priest in that setting was '*in persona Christi*,'' or, as

Thomas Aquinas put it, he knows the confession "not as man, but as God knows it." No matter how modern and worldly a priest Hugh considered himself to be, this kinship with Christ, this closeness, was thrilling to him. He didn't want to violate or lose it.

But as he lay in bed that night, it wasn't the face of his Savior that he saw—it was the nervous, doomed little figure of Teddy Valuckas spilling the beans on Leavenworth Street. And then it was Anibel, dear Anibel, and her reminder of the curiously unstolen Whistler that kept him awake and wondering.

CHAPTER 4

Father Hugh Osgood's love of sports went all the way back to his young boyhood. By age 10 or 11, he could reliably be found organizing the neighborhood boys and even some of the girls into baseball or football games, usually in the chestnut tree shade of the playground at Driggs School. In high school, he was a good left-handed pitcher and a long-range set-shot artist on the basketball team who later led his pretty decent seminary team in scoring. In all the team sports, he prided himself on knowing the rules and not making mistakes. The coaches couldn't wait to make him captain.

Golf began early, too. Hugh's dad had an old set of hickory-shafted clubs that he no longer had any use for, he not possessing what he called "the temperament for the game." The clubs were right-handed and way too long for Hugh, but he went out and started practicing with them right away, whacking away at the few yellowing old balls his father had left in a shag bag. Before long, he'd found several other would-be golfers who were roughly his age, including Danny Gill, and they began to play together. Their routine was simple and sweet. Carrying their clubs, they'd walk from their neighborhood to Exchange Place downtown, where all the city bus routes converged. They'd board the Hamilton Avenue bus and take it all the way out to East Mountain, where they'd get off and walk up to the city's municipal course. There, a boy could play 9 holes for 50 cents and 18 for a dollar—and sometimes a friendly starter would, with a wink, let them tee off for free.

Whether he was playing with others or by himself, Hugh

loved the game. It was difficult to learn, but he could be patient. It required both routine and imagination, a combination he found intriguing. But most of all he just liked being out on the course, on its long stretches of sun-dappled fairway and fragrant, close-cropped greens. And if he could hit an occasional excellent shot or hear a long putt rattle into the cup, well that was good enough for him.

So who could blame him for saying yes when, earlier that spring of 1955, a small committee came to visit and offered him a gratis golf membership at the posh Country Club of Waterbury? Hugh had been shocked by the offer. Having his name on a locker at the country club was not something that a kid with his background ever dared aspire to. If you came out of a row of three-family houses in Waterbury, as Hugh did, you were expected to play at East Mountain and perhaps one day join the men's association there. That was where the cops, firemen and mailmen, like his dad, played and had a beer or two after the round. For Hugh, the country club was an emerald oasis way out on the city's west side, practically in the country, a place where they drank cocktails rather than beer. Even after he'd come back to town to his post at the Immaculate, he'd thought of the club as unattainable and inappropriate, like an MG convertible or a date with Ava Gardner. Still, anytime he'd come out for a reception following a wedding or funeral he found himself staring out at the first tee and fairway from the big clubhouse windows. He longed to play there. And then after he finally did inveigle his way into playing a few rounds—several of the Gills were members—he only fell ever more desperately under its spell. So when the committee, led by old Waterbury blueblood Sandy Jones, asked him to join, it was almost like a dream come true.

Not that he gave his assent right away. He first had to establish that there'd been precedent for such an offer; he found that indeed the club had long held a spot open for a local Protestant minister, a Catholic priest and the mayor of the city. He then went on bended knee to Msgr. Shutt, an old athlete himself, who rather kindly and unexpectedly concluded that Hugh's mingling with

Waterbury's elite might do the church some good. So, yes, he accepted. And if anyone objected to his playing golf—or playing a hand or two of cards in the clubhouse afterwards, for that matter—he'd just say he'd been brought in to keep his otherwise straying fellow members honest, and clean of word, thought and deed.

Because of his irregular schedule and never-on-Sunday status, Hugh was unable to become part of a regular group. When he was approached by Sandy Jones to join a foursome that would play every Tuesday afternoon, Hugh demurred, even though it had been Jones who'd most wanted to give him his membership, and he'd felt, to some degree, beholden. Perhaps for that reason, whenever Jones subsequently called him in search of a fourth, which was often, he tended to say yes, if he could. Hugh sensed a curious neediness in Jones' voice and didn't want to appear ungrateful.

Sandy Jones was a strange cat. He was a year or two over 60, colored his hair jet black, had never married, came from a prominent, privileged Waterbury family and was at one time, if no longer, a legitimate championship golfer. He was nominally an attorney, but these days he spent most of his time at the club, where his allegiance was legendary. It was said that he'd personally kept the operation afloat with infusions of cash during the dark days of the Depression—and ever since he'd assumed an unpleasant, unofficial and nearly dictatorial role in the running of things there, both out on the course and in the clubhouse. At present, he was busy keeping the club from putting in a swimming pool (he called the idea "vulgar"), despite the wishes of a new generation of postwar parents with small children.

Hugh had heard stories about Jones's darker side as well. For one thing, he drank to excess, sometimes right out of the bottle, which is a special kind of drinking. A few years back, the club had commissioned a portrait of Jones as a way of thanking him for his past support. The painting, which Hugh thought captured Jones's liver lips and furtive brow, now hung by the fireplace in the club's men-only Grill Room—not because it was a place of prominence, which is what they'd told Jones, but because it was where he'd often relieved himself late in the evening when he was too drunk and uncaring to make it all the way to the men's room. He could be a bully, too. There was the time he ran into the club's new golf pro on his first day on the job and demanded the young man give him his wristwatch. He then laid the watch flat and face up on the first tee, placed a golf ball on it, and hit the ball off it with a full 3-iron swing. No one had the nerve to tell him that he'd hit the ball but damaged the watch, too, and that a collection had to be taken up to buy the pro a new one. Even more unpleasantly, Jones insisted on being Santa Claus at the club's annual Christmas brunch. His portrayal was far from convincing and many children reported they'd felt uncomfortable sitting on his lap, that he smelled like cigarettes, and that they didn't like the way he squeezed and bounced them. It left everyone with a dirty, even angry, feeling, which was far from the intention. Finally, there were the reports of Jones's collection of "blue" movies, the crudest sort of pornography, which he'd screen at home in Waterbury for drinking buddies and a stray soul or two he'd haul in from the street or a downtown bar. Could there have been even darker secrets? Hugh had heard there were, but he wasn't inclined to dig.

The other two who usually made up the foursome had their own peculiar ties to Jones. Newt Harding was widely known as Jones' amiable pigeon, someone who could always be counted on to do his master's bidding and never beat him at either golf or cards. The third, Sam Pepe, a former caddie and scratch golfer, was the club's first Italian member. His admission had apparently been ramrodded through by Jones, who thus felt entitled to refer to him as "the Wop" or otherwise disparage him ("He's our resident little Italian," Jones had said more than once. "He could shorten his name but he couldn't shorten his nose."). Pepe, like racial barrier breakers everywhere, took it all with a patient, pained smile and an inner pledge to someday get revenge.

Even so, even with this load of ugly baggage, Hugh had frequently said yes to joining Jones for a round of golf. He soon began wondering why. For one thing, he reasoned, the requests were coming from the club's most prominent member, one of the city's supposed social elites of whom Msgr. Shutt had spoken. He thought it would have been rude to say no. In fact, how *could* he say no? If he wanted to justify it, he could tell himself that he would be like a missionary who'd bring light into Jones's rough routines. He could look for quiet, priestly ways to redirect the older man's inclinations—not always possible after he'd had a few. But these justifications were hopelessly weak. Hugh saw soon and plainly that joining the club had been an impulsive mistake. He'd succumbed to flattery and a free offer. He began looking for ways of leaving. The golf was great, and so were many of the members, but no matter which way you looked at it, he was the odd man out. He should have seen it coming.

Nonetheless, he was still in attendance late on a Thursday afternoon in mid-May, joined with Jones, Harding and Pepe deep into a round of setback played for cigarette stakes, when the bartender came over with the bulletin he'd just heard on the radio: arrests had been made in the Wheeler art theft and murder case. The card game stopped dead.

"Who were they?" Hugh asked. It was news he hadn't been expecting.

"Two guys, local fish," the bartender said. "I didn't catch the names. They sounded like Frenchmen to me."

Even based on these few descriptives, Hugh didn't think they sounded like art thieves. He was still—the days by now turning into weeks—holding the Valuckas card, unsure of how and when (and if) to use it. He now thought the moment might be coming soon.

"I hope they hang them," Jones said loudly to the whole room. "For these low-lifes to walk into the Wheelers like that—a family that's done so much for this city—and remove things from the very walls—it's such a violation. It's such an overt crime. It simply can't be tolerated."

The 15 or so other members at surrounding tables sat in silent nodding agreement. Jones was old-line Waterbury, in his milieu, sticking up for his kind. Fair enough, thought Hugh. Jones was a neighbor and old friend of the Wheelers, probably beginning in boyhood. In this case he was entitled to his anger, but Hugh didn't want to stick around as he drank himself into a rage. Citing a Catechism class, which he'd now have to drop in on, he excused himself from the game and drove back to the rectory to give Dan a call.

◆ ◆ ◆

Dan was at his newsroom desk. Hugh spoke quietly on the rectory's communal phone, the extension located in the pantry. Dan had already written most of the next day's story on the arrests and was now just waiting for a couple of calls to be returned. He was ready to talk it over. In fact, he liked talking about the case with others; he could speculate in ways he could never do in the newspaper. He and Hugh had spoken a few times in recent weeks, so Dan knew of his old friend's interest in the case hadn't waned. He thought Hugh's continuing fascination came from his being cooped up in the rectory so much of the time. A juicy crime might allow him some vicarious enjoyment. Obviously, Hugh hadn't told him anything about Valuckas, not even as much as he'd told Anibel.

"This is definitely not where my reporting was leading," Dan said in response to Hugh's question. "These guys are known small-time losers. All brawn. No ambition."

"Where *is* your reporting leading?" Hugh asked.

"Higher up. I've been talking to people in the art world. They tend to think it could be organized crime or international thievery of some kind, but that somewhere in the mix there's an art expert and also someone with knowledge of the Wheelers' holdings."

"Well, it's not like they kept them hidden," Hugh said. "The milkman probably saw the Monets through the window when he walked by every morning."

"I like that, Hugh. I'll have to talk to the milkman, and maybe the dry cleaning guy, too. In fact, it could even be the newspaper boy. I'll have to check my sources in the circulation department."

Hugh smiled. The banter was vastly preferable to the overprivileged small talk of the Grill Room.

"So these guys they arrested couldn't be part of it at any level?"

"I don't know. I suppose they could be, as drivers or something like that. But they've charged them with felony theft, as if they were the main perpetrators. I don't see that being the case."

"Maybe they think they can get them to talk and name bigger names."

"Yeah, no doubt," Dan said. "But there's also something else."

"What's that?"

"This is an odd-numbered year, an election year for the mayor, and this is a crime that's caught everyone's attention and that needs to be solved. The police department needs to show that it's alert and functioning. If you can announce these arrests and then drag your feet with delays, stays and procedure, it can get you right through to November and maybe even beyond."

"So cynical," said Hugh. "It takes my breath away."

"I blame it on the newsroom water cooler," said Dan. "Before long in here you begin to distrust even your own motives."

Hugh was ready to sign off and get to his Catechism class, but Dan had something else to add.

"You should know that my mother has in mind a 30th birthday party for me," he said with a warning tone.

"That should be lovely," said Hugh.

"Yes, it will be that. You'll of course get a formal invitation in the mail, and be expected to RSVP promptly, but I wanted you to know it's to be a joint celebration."

"I'm to be honored, too?"

"Not only that."

"What?"

"Anibel's coming. Mom didn't want to leave her out. She's

turning 30, too."

"Wow, a big bash then," Hugh said, taken aback a little.

"Seems so."

"Maybe with a review of old times?"

"That is a Gill specialty, so maybe more like a decade-by-decade panorama."

"Alright then, Danny. I'm in. Sign me up as the life of the party."

◆ ◆ ◆

Three weeks later, Hugh, Dan and Anibel sprawled on the Gills' rear screen porch, the last partygoers left at the end of the long birthday night. Above and below them on the hill, the city slept, but the three honorees were at last fully relaxed and enjoying each other's company too much to call it quits. One more glass, they'd agreed. Last call. Now, as Dan came to the end of a long anecdote regarding an old Crosby classmate who turned out to be an arsonist, Hugh raised his glass.

"When was the last time the three of us were together—I mean just us three?" he asked, with the tiniest hint of a slur in his voice. "It seems like forever."

"I don't know, high school?" answered Dan.

"A little later than that," suggested Anibel. "I can clearly picture us getting together in Becker's back room just before you both went overseas. October 1943."

"Drinking Rheingolds," Dan remembered.

"Illegally," added Anibel.

"But Becker insisted that if we were old enough to risk our lives in a war, we were old enough to have a beer," said Hugh.

"They were on him, too," said Dan. "He was a guilt-stricken German."

"I guess he thought there was something risky about me going off to Smith College, too," said Anibel.

They laughed and then fell silent.

"We were lucky," said Dan.

A longer silence as each thought about what that meant.

The party, as expertly planned and stage-managed by Dan's mother, had gone well. The guest list had been impressively complete, with representatives from family, early childhood, high school, current friends, work associates and neighbors in attendance. There'd been champagne, crème de menthe parfaits and music from a live jazz combo. The speeches were brief and not too bad. Dr. Gill read a funny telegram from Anibel's parents, who'd moved away up to Maine following her dad's retirement. Kind acknowledgement of Hugh's late parents had been made by longtime neighbor Herb Sands, who lived midway between the Gills' big place and the Osgoods' far more modest triple-decker and knew both families well. There'd been singing, with Dan's sister, Aggie, at the piano, and even a couple of magic tricks from one of the young nephews.

And now it was all over except for the big, broad, unknowable future that lay before all three of them. There'd been pride and admiration expressed in what they'd accomplished already during the war and more recently as young pillars of journalism, high culture and the Church. But the expectations of what they might still achieve—*should* achieve—formed a quietly insistent companion theme, one that certainly could have dominated the evening had it not been for a certain art-theft-and-murder case, which Dan now brought up.

"I've never heard so many Wheeler takes as I heard tonight," he said.

"People have their own theories?" Hugh asked with mock innocence.

"Oh, yes. Everyone's an expert, as you are yourself. Tonight I heard, among many others, that it was the work of a resentful, little known wing of the Wheeler family, or it had to be the Masons with the loot now stashed in their temple downtown, or maybe it was a band of beret-wearing French nationalists bent on reclaiming the paintings for their homeland."

"All very helpful, I'm sure" said Anibel. She was swirling

Chablis in one of the thick red goblets—"Depression glass," they were beginning to call it—that Dan's mother had set out in an effort to evoke younger days.

"Maybe the mastermind was in the room," Hugh suggested. "Right there in plain view, laughing and singing with the rest of us."

"We needed Miss Marple to ferret him out," said Anibel.

"Actually, I'm surprised your mother didn't think to invite a private detective," said Hugh. "It would have made the party, to gather all the guests in a room for questioning."

"You laugh, but anything is probably helpful at this point," Dan said.

"So no one believes the case has actually been solved?" Anibel asked.

"No. I think the unofficial attitude is that it's been solved until something better comes along."

Hugh's moment was upon him.

"In that case," he said, "I think I may have something better."

Almost from the time he'd first heard about the birthday party from Dan, he'd sensed that it would turn out to be the occasion at which he'd tell these two the story of Teddy Valuckas and open up all the messy baggage that came with him. He was eager to share the weight of it. Somewhere in the swirl of the past couple of months, he'd convinced himself, although not without considerable guilt, that it would be possible, and professionally and ethically acceptable, for him to tell all: Valuckas hadn't confessed, hadn't made an Act of Contrition, hadn't done penance, and hadn't even clearly defined his role in the crime, if he actually had a role at all. Those arguments, in just that order, had been rolling around in Hugh's head for over a month. Now, on the Gill's screen porch, with just the faintest light beginning to show in the eastern sky, he looked up to see Dan and Anibel staring at him with the greatest possible anticipation.

"You're my most trusted friends in the world, and you always have been, so please bear with me," he said. "I don't know what it all adds up to, if anything, or where it leads, if anywhere, but I have a story to tell you. Stay up another few minutes and hear me out."

And with that, Hugh at last, before the eyes of God, unburdened himself.

CHAPTER 5

Two weeks later, Hugh Osgood once again awoke out of a troubled sleep. Again, he'd been in a soaring Gothic chamber where a panel of judges was deciding his fate. This time they were hooded and faceless, but like always they were out for his hide. He knew he'd done something wrong, but he wasn't sure what it was. Pressing in on him, they asked questions he couldn't answer, and he kept repeating, "It was all a mistake, it was all a mistake," until finally he woke up. Another terrible, guilt-ridden dream. Now, lying on his back in his bed, he stared up at the ceiling and transitioned to the real-life punishments he felt certain would be coming his way once all was known about his Valuckas revelation: defrocking, excommunication, a life of shame. Even worse, on a June night with too much scotch in his belly, he'd pulled Dan and Anibel into what might turn out to be a deadly game. Dan was now quietly looking into Teddy Valuckas and who knew what else. Anibel was doubling down on her new friendship with the Wheelers, trying to determine who else might have shown a special interest in the stolen paintings. Both had sworn secrecy, but Hugh had seen that both were excited by the story and their special place in it. They were eager to become more involved, Danny of course for professional reasons, but Anibel, too. She compared it to the Hardy Boys and Nancy Drew. She wasn't thinking of the chauffeur's bullet-torn body wrapped up alongside the Naugatuck River.

Hugh had kept his windows open during the warm summer night and now, as he lay in bed, he heard the first stirrings of the new day on and around the Waterbury Green. A few cars and trucks rumbled by on West Main Street, the street sweeper, Mr. Sills, pushed his squeaky-wheeled bin along the gutter, the bell at St. John's tolled five times, then, 30 seconds later, as if in answer, the deeper, more distant train station bell struck the hour. Soon it would be time for Hugh to rise and prepare for early mass, but before he did that, he wanted to flush out the bad dreams and clear his head. As always, he went to the familiar places, the memories that persisted and even grew more vivid over time. For some, such early-morning thoughts were of old girlfriends, or athletic exploits, or the slow parade of rooms in a childhood house, but not for Hugh. Like so many other men and women of a certain age lying awake in their beds all over the world on that morning in early July 1955, his thoughts, private and rarely spoken, turned yet again to the war.

Upon his enlistment with Dan in 1943, he'd said his goodbyes and, following basic training, was ordered to Camp Toccoa, Georgia, for paratrooper school and assignment to the 11th Airborne Division. Before he knew it, he was routinely jumping out of airplanes. The following April, he was sent to California and then a month later on to New Guinea for still more training and then, finally, to the battles for the Philippines. There, he and all the other so-called "Angels" would be fighting the Japanese as part of MacArthur's famous earlier promise to "return."

With the 11th, Hugh saw plenty of both infantry and paratrooper action. He took part in the invasions of Leyte and Luzon, fought in pitched combat south of Manila and dropped into battle zones both day and night. He barely had time to breathe. He zig-zagged up a beach as shells explode around him, parachuted onto brutal terrain that killed or injured dozens of his fellow paratroopers, and watched in horror as flamethrowers routed screaming Japanese from their bunkers. At times, he felt surrounded by bad luck, injury and death. He wondered if this was where his life would end, with so little written on his ledger and no idea of what the future might have held for him. He wondered, too, if this was the best men could do, to put on uniforms and day after day throw themselves into battle. Still, he did it. He was a brave soldier. Eventually, he experienced enough to earn himself a Purple Heart, Bronze Star and Philippines Liberation Medal.

But it was one epic operation early in 1945, toward the end of his hitch, that lifted his sights and changed his life. As the Japanese began to lose ground in the Pacific, they took their anger and frustration out on those they'd captured along the way. Among these were teachers, businessmen, foreign government workers, clergy, seminarians and nuns—the so-called "enemy civilians" whose home countries were at odds with the Japanese effort. At first these thousands were warned and watched and restricted in their travel, then they were rounded up and put into camps, and finally, in many cases, as the Japanese grew panicky, they began to be tortured and starved to death.

One of the most notorious of these camps was Los Banos, located 20 miles behind enemy lines in the Philippines' Laguna Province. When they first started moving people in, the Japanese publicly described Los Banos as "an ideal health resort noted for its hot springs" and promised that those held there would have the benefit of fresh air as well as fresh meat and vegetables. Whatever their early stated intentions, by the end of 1944 the camp had turned into a prison, serving one "meal" a day, consisting of inedible *palay*, or unhusked rice. The prisoners, who'd already been in captivity for months or years, began dying more quickly than the gravediggers could bury them.

Hugh Osgood was part of the operation that would, in one lightning strike, liberate the prisoners of Los Banos. With exquisite planning, training, timing and the help of local militia, the combined forces of the 511th Parachute Infantry Regiment, 188th Glider Infantry Division and 672nd Amphibian Tractor Battalion swept into the camp early on the morning of February 23, 1945. Hugh parachuted with 150 others into a small drop zone marked by green smoke from flares set by advance scouts, rendezvoused with a local guerilla unit, quickly and brutally neutralized the Japanese guards and secured the internees. By day's end, the operation had rescued and evacuated all 2,147 prisoners—every one of them—without a single death or serious injury reported among them. It would turn out to be one of the greatest such rescues in military history.

Now, lying undisturbed in his rectory bed, his hands clasped behind his head, Hugh savored the rest of the story, as he often did before beginning a new day. As the camp was held securely at its perimeters, the prisoners were ferried out in dozens of amphibious tractors. Some objected to being moved but changed their minds when the Americans began setting their barracks on fire. The rescue took many hours. It was known that 8,000-10,000 Japanese soldiers were bivouacked nearby, but they never appeared. As the long day's light began to fade, Hugh hopped onto one of the last amtracs to leave and settled in next to one of the detainees, a young teaching Brother from the De La Salle order, for the ride over land and then water to safety. Sharing a cigarette between them and feeling the special intimacy sometimes shared by strangers surrounded by danger, the two began to talk.

At Hugh's urging, the priest spoke first of the conditions in the camp, where he'd spent the last six months. At the beginning, it hadn't been too bad, he said. Each inmate had a 10' by 14' space of his own and there was adequate food and fresh water.

"They allowed the priests and nuns to occupy their own section of the yard," he told Hugh. "We could celebrate mass and preach sermons of encouragement. Our compound came to be called the Vatican."

"Did the others resent it?" Hugh asked.

"I don't think so, although our ground was a little higher up. They made jokes about that, too, but we didn't get any special privileges, except . . ."

"Except what?"

"Somehow we came into possession of a supply of corned beef, which we guarded jealously. We carved off little bits on special occasions. To us, it was like candy."

"So not too bad?"

"It got very bad. As the Japs realized they weren't going to win the war, they began to take it out on us with isolation and beatings, and then a new boss came in—Konishi."

"What was he like?"

"Small, arrogant, brutal—actually sadistic, I think. Under his rule, Los Banos quickly became a prison, the only word for it, with punishments and vastly reduced food and water. There was no care for the sick or injured and no effort at sanitation. We were forced to live in our own filth. Many died."

"But now many have been rescued, too," said Hugh, gesturing toward the interior of the amtrac, in which 30 or 40 former captives were riding to freedom.

"Yes, of course," replied the Lasallian. "This is all so new. It seems like a miracle. When I saw you and the others floating down from heaven this morning, I fell to my knees in thanks."

He paused. Hugh realized that he and this filthy, emaciated, world-weary figure before him were not much different in age.

"Some of them came very close to making it out alive," the Lasallian continued. "Some of the best among us."

Then, with the amtrac bouncing along the rutted road and the sounds of nearby conversations rising and falling, he told the story of Old Joe Mulry.

Father Joseph A. Mulry, S.J., was a New Yorker and an instructor at Fordham who'd come out to the Philippines in the 1920s to teach poetry and rhetoric at Ateneo, the Jesuit University in Manila. He quickly became a star on campus, not only for his work in the classroom, but also for his inspiring role in social justice crusades, especially among farmers, and the revitalization of the Catholic press and the Catholic voice. He also groomed certain of his students for leadership roles after they graduated. "Mulry's Boys" became known for their poise, persuasive speaking ability and intellectual rigor.

"At Los Banos, Father Mulry was billeted with the other Jesuits in Barrack 19," the Lasallian said, "and at some point, when things got really bad and people were despairing, his superiors came to the remarkable conclusion that others in the camp might benefit in many ways if he were to conduct a lecture series on Shakespeare."

Hugh laughed out loud, a quick snort, but the Lasallian's expression was unchanged.

"Our barrack was about 200 yards away from No. 19, so on the evenings when Joe Mulry's lectures were scheduled, we'd crawl on our bellies at the risk of our lives to hear them. He'd be sitting there on a bamboo mat, shadow and light on his face, the illumination coming from a coconut shell filled with oil. A lighted wick was floating on top of the oil. It was the only light in the barracks because American planes sometimes flew overhead and the whole camp was under orders to maintain a strict black-out. Anyway, Old Joe lectured brilliantly and with great humor and understanding on Hamlet, Macbeth and King Lear. Surreal, yes, but it meant everything to us to be able to hear this, not only to get through another night in the camp but to actually feel lifted up and ennobled, even as we crawled back through the mud to our cots."

"He didn't make it out?" Hugh asked after a moment.

"He died about a month ago. Typically, he'd been giving his ration of food to others, and then one night he became very ill, and despite the very best efforts to save him he was dead within hours. They said it was stomach problems, bleeding ulcers, but basically he starved to death. He was 55."

With that, the Lasallian ended his story. He stared straight ahead for a minute or two and then collapsed directly into sleep, resting his head on Hugh's shoulder.

Hugh wanted to sleep, too, and deeply. The events of the day had finally caught up with him. But first he had to contend with a host of other thoughts and feelings. Somewhere within the Lasallian's narrative Hugh began to hear another voice as well, a calling out to him, as strange and frightening as anything the war had to offer. He was weary and hungry, and in many ways a lonely, searching, parentless, rudderless 20-year-old in a remote jungle at the end of the world, but the voice was clear and strong enough to turn him upside down. He knew right away what it was. He was getting the call. He'd always heard about it, but now he was getting it himself. There was a reason why the Lasallian had told him the story. Men could do better than endlessly provoke bloodshed upon one another. There was still room for light in the world if only people could be persuaded to see and welcome it. When Hugh got back home, if he got there in one piece, he'd follow the lead of Old Joe Mulry, take the torch from him, and put his kind of purpose and meaning—actual meaning, actual doing—into his life, too.

Of course, as he'd grown comfortable with that decision, he'd considered his situation with Anibel, too. He knew she was waiting for him. He'd written her often and gotten letters in return. She wrote about her life on campus, describing how even Smith College had become militarized for the war effort, calling itself U.S.S. Northampton and becoming the official training ground for the country's first women naval officers, the WAVES. Anibel wrote colorfully and at length about other aspects of homefront life, too, describing rationing, War Bond rallies and deaths and injuries among the boys who'd signed up from Crosby. Hugh appreciated the news from home, but as time went on, he began to worry about his ability to live up to Anibel. She sounded so assured and mature. He worried that her time in college was putting her way out ahead of him in so many important ways, and that she deserved, and maybe even needed, a lot more than he could give her. Doubt fed upon doubt. She was a mature woman, he was a kid in a helmet. He couldn't believe that anyone would want to love him so much. And then God spoke to him. Years later, he wondered if that's what made the sudden tumble into the religious life so appealing. With the Church, he'd be able to join an orderly family that would feed and shelter him, overlook his flaws and allow him to grow on his own terms. He liked to think he'd swum toward Christ with a pure heart, but maybe he was simply not ready for the life of responsibilities and real-world decisions that otherwise awaited him. When the time finally came for them to talk in person, his description to Anibel of his calling and his decision to answer it came across as something beyond his ability to reverse. He wasn't trying to be unfeeling, but he never really allowed her to have a say or describe to him how they might still grow together—how he might go to college and take things as they came. He didn't give her side of things enough credit, or any credit at all. He didn't respect her or understand how much he was hurting her. He told her he loved her but that there was now something else he loved more, something that couldn't be denied. He thought she would eventually understand, but she never did.

◆ ◆ ◆

At breakfast later that morning, Hugh spread out the paper and read Danny's latest dispatch. He'd written something on the case a couple of times a week, always advancing the story but sometimes not by very much. Today's was a take on art insurance and the need for it in an accelerating market. He polled experts in New York and Hartford, and of course Anibel, to conclude that the old carefree days were gone, that artworks, beyond their aesthetic value, were a hot investment commodity and that insurance and security were now necessities. "You can't just hang a painting in your living room and enjoy it," he quoted one expert as saying. "You've got to know its value, insure it properly, keep it secure, maybe even hide it away or use a replica. You've got to assume the bad guys are out there watching."

Hugh was wondering how many in the newspaper's circulation area would have to change their habits because of the article when Mrs. Dunn interrupted his thoughts to tell him he had a phone call from the author himself. He went into the pantry to take it.

"I just wanted to let you know I've had a breakthrough on Valuckas," Dan said. "I figured you should be the first to know."

"Thank you," said Hugh, looking around to see if anyone was nearby. "I'm not sure this is the wisest way to tell me."

"Want to talk later?"

"No, go ahead."

"Well, I couldn't get anywhere with his widow, as I think I already told you. She was scared to death about something and wouldn't talk. This made me very suspicious, of course, so I kept an eye on her. I eventually saw that she spent a huge amount of time with her next-door neighbor who I found out was her sister-in-law, also a widow named Valuckas, first name of June. Hubby died in Korea."

Dan sounded like he was reading from his notes.

"And?"

"I made sure I bumped into June one day at the bus stop, I started a friendly conversation with her and discovered that she *loves* to talk. Wouldn't stop talking, in fact."

"She sounds like her brother-in-law. Teddy liked to talk, too."

"Well, one thing led to another. One minute we're talking about rationing and the cost of a bus ride and the next she'd telling me how Thomas Murphy, the chauffeur at the Wheelers, used to hire Teddy for heavy-lifting odd jobs he couldn't handle himself. And not only that, but that he also used to hire Pelletier and Roy, the two guys the cops arrested."

Hugh began to shift the puzzle pieces.

"So Murphy was the mastermind?" he asked.

"I certainly don't think so," said Dan.

"He was more like the host."

"Yeah."

"The manager."

"Exactly. He took orders from above and welcomed in the muscle, although why they needed all the help taking down some paintings I don't know."

"And one of them killed Murphy?"

"Probably your guy."

"He's not my guy," said Hugh.

There was a pause in the conversation. Hugh heard two of his fellow priests, Ferraro and Fox, walk down the hall and out the front door. In the kitchen, Mrs. Dunn noisily ran the breakfast dishes through the suds.

"So how did Teddy Valuckas really die?" Hugh asked.

"That's what I have to find out next," Dan said. "June is working on it."

"You're kidding me! She knows you're a reporter?"

"Yes, and she'd excited about it. She says her sister-in-law, Peggy, hasn't really spoken about it at all but she thinks she can get it out of her."

"The obituary said 'natural causes.'"

"Yeah, well, that's just obit talk. It could mean anything. It's like when an obit says someone 'died suddenly.' Everyone dies suddenly. One second you're alive, the next you're dead. It bothers me every time I read it."

"Well, thanks for filling me in," said Hugh, "although maybe next time we should meet in a coffee shop or on a park bench."

"Like a spy novel."

"Yeah."

"Okay, Hugh, I thought you'd want to know. And, by the way, one more thing about Valuckas."

"What's that?"

"He's definitely your guy."

That evening, Dan was at his desk in the newsroom when a package arrived for him. The receptionist had found it leaning against a wall just inside the building's front door. It was tube-shaped, wrapped in brown paper, tied up with twine and addressed to him in a blocky, all-caps style. Could it be an early 1956 calendar? A pin-up? Marilyn Monroe? Dan slit the package down one side with his penknife and slowly unfurled what was inside. Yes, a pin-up of a very special sort—Manet's "The Race Horses in the Bois de Boulogne," cut just a tiny bit crudely from its frame but otherwise unharmed. Using his glue pot, scissors and a few city directories, he flattened out the canvas on his desk and stared down at it. The horses and jockeys were painted as if by someone who'd never seen an actual race, or an actual horse—very much in the unrealistic style of an old English sporting print. Not so far removed from a cave painting. But here it was, back from its thrilling trip in and out of thieving hands. Dan stared some more before he called the police. He wondered what it meant when the fish started jumping into the boat.

CHAPTER 6

"The game is afoot, chillun!"

Anibel, doing her best impression of a Georgia peach, slipped into the booth next to Dan and across from Hugh.

"I'm not sure if that's Shakespeare or Sherlock," she continued, a little out of breath and perspiring after the brisk walk over from her office, "but I do think we're finally getting somewhere. Or at least Dan is." She smiled. "How's that for a table setter?"

The men made their friendly hellos to her. The three were gathered for lunch at the rear of the bar room of the popular downtown restaurant, Diorio's, where the high-backed bankers booths had long allowed a measure of privacy, and not only to bankers. Over the preceding weeks they'd often met in twos and communicated via telephone and hastily scribbled notes, but this was the first time all three had gotten together since the birthday bash and Hugh's revelation back in June. Now it was the very hot and humid first week of August. Dan's big story on Teddy Valuckas had just appeared. It tied him in with Pelletier and Roy as doing occasional chores together at the Wheeler residence, questioned the manner of his death, and pointed out that, with the return of the Manet, the two men in jail—still held without bail—could hardly be the only ones responsible for the original theft. There was a growing sense that the whole criminal enterprise might soon collapse. It seemed like a good time to regroup.

"I was just telling Dan what a tremendous leap forward that story was," said Hugh. "It made me feel I was right to come forward about Valuckas."

"I think it was the key that might unlock this whole thing," Dan said. "The cops might have gotten their two guys to talk —they probably would have eventually—but this really opens things up."

"And thanks for keeping me way in the background," Hugh said.

"Invisible, really, to anyone but us," said Anibel.

"The holy ghost," said Dan, which made them all laugh.

"The police must really be swarming now," said Anibel after a pause.

"They are, and some state cops are in on it now, too," said Dan. "They'll make life miserable for Teddy's widow, but I'm not sure how much she actually knows. She comes home one afternoon to find her husband lying on the couch, dead of an apparent heart attack. No signs of violence. No reason to be suspicious. She knows he's not an angel and that Murphy hired him for odd jobs, but that's the extent of it. She buries him, mourns with her kids, protects them by keeping her mouth shut, and that's that."

"Now they'll unbury him," said Hugh.

"I think so," said Dan. "They've applied for a court order to dig him up and perform a proper autopsy."

The waiter brought their bowls of Italian-style gazpacho and a basket of bread. Diorio's famous cold soup and a glass of ice water served well against the summer heat.

"Any theories on the return of the Manet?" Anibel asked.

"None," said Dan. "Lots of ill-informed conjecture but nothing I've heard that rises to the level of a theory. Hugh here is a good one for theories, though. Any ideas?"

As Anibel and Dan looked at him from across the table, Hugh was suddenly aware that they were now a couple. There was a glow in their smiling faces, and once he saw that, it was easy to pick up on the other things—their relaxed give and take, the ease with which they sat so close together, and now Dan was literally buttering Anibel's bread. He replayed how she'd slid so naturally into the booth next to Dan. Could she have playfully touched his elbow as she'd done so? He wondered how many times they'd met without him since he'd last seen them together. The game truly *was* afoot.

"Hugh?"

It was Dan, still waiting for an answer.

"Sorry, just theorizing," said Hugh, returning a bit dizzily to the question at hand. "What could cause the thieves to return one of the paintings? I have no idea. Maybe they just wanted the frame. Or maybe it was an aesthetic judgment. They didn't like the Manet. Remember, there was another painting they never even took off the Wheelers' wall."

"Nice try, but, no, I don't think so," said Dan. "I've considered misdirection or even just a perverse wish to be caught or turn the whole thing into a game. But none of that really adds up, either."

"Well, I can tell you that the Wheelers are happy to have the painting back—or will be once they actually get it," said Anibel.

"You've been spending lots of time with Seth and Alice, I take it?" said Hugh, referring to the senior Wheelers.

"I've offered them the benefit of my expertise," she said. "And they're steeped in the history of their family, which I find fascinating. They see themselves as the custodians of everything —the art and history, the traditions, the way of life. Their kids have grown up and left the nest and don't seem to care nearly as much."

"Nineteenth century versus twentieth," said Hugh.

"They can see the day coming when they'll have to sell off everything—the paintings, the furniture, the house—and cash it out among all the relations."

"That'll make some museums happy."

"And some Wheelers, too, but not Seth and Alice."

"And how have they reacted to the whole thing?" Hugh asked.

"As Dan knows, they've cooperated completely with the police and are shocked by the murder of their man Murphy, but overall they're bemoaning the modern world and want to get out of Waterbury. They said the city's big industrial days are pretty much played out at this point. No reason to stick around."

"The last old-money WASP leaving town be sure to turn out the lights," said Dan.

"They moved into the house 12 years ago, when Seth's dad, Burton, the great collector, passed away. I get the feeling they've never changed anything out of respect for him. Not only did the paintings remain in place—they told me they never moved them—but the same with the furniture, the draperies, the kitchen appliances. They're probably ready to make a fresh start in the suburbs.

"Also, I was wondering who might have been familiar with the house and paintings," Anibel continued, "so I managed to get my hands on the Wheelers' invitation list for their annual Christmas party."

"Any surprises?" asked Hugh.

"Not really. Hart, Jones, Hyde, Burr, Taft, Todd—the usual gang of one-syllable names."

"All now in genteel decline," said Dan. "Soon there won't be anyone left in the city but the widows and ne'er-do-wells."

"The Episcopalians are always the first to bail," said Hugh with a chuckle, and then he asked Anibel if she had any theories about why the Manet had been returned.

"Guilt, maybe? Fear? Someone overcome by the enormity and possible consequences of what's he's done?"

"Who now wants to undo everything?" said Hugh.

"Exactly. And hope that everyone will just sort of forget about the whole thing."

"Which would seem to leave out the professionals as suspects," said Hugh.

"One would think."

"Which would be a change from earlier thinking."

"Yes," said Dan. "It's not an international art-theft ring. Can't be. Not with the painting coming back."

There was no time for lingering on this busy workday.

Following a brief gossipy flurry devoted to other things and an agreement to get together again soon or as warranted, the three of them left Diorio's and walked up Bank Street and down Grand Street together. As Dan continued on to the newspaper office, Anibel and Hugh turned down Leavenworth toward the Green.

"This may be none of my business," began Hugh as they got halfway down the block.

"That means it's definitely not your business at all."

Still, she looked at him expectantly.

"It's you and Dan," he said. "There's been a change. You're . . ."

He faltered.

"Together, yes," said Anibel. "Is it that obvious? We've been spending more and more time together this summer, and we've found we like each other very much and possibly, probably, always have. We're giving it a try."

They walked awhile in silence. Hugh wanted to say something even though the priest in him was telling him to shut up.

"I –" Hugh began, not quite knowing where he was headed, but Anibel interrupted, putting a hand on his forearm and stopping them both on the sidewalk.

"Hugh, I'll never be over you, but I'm over you," she said. "I have to be. Otherwise it's impossible. I never imagined we'd end up back home, all tossed together like this."

"I know. I understand. I don't mind saying that I've had to bury my feelings about you so many times, but I knew I'd never act on them."

"Nor would I want you to. You're a good priest, Hugh."

"I hope so. Anyway, you have a good man in Dan."

"Yeah, he's great. He's a forward thinker, I love the way he looks and talks, and he's riding high right now. And we've got a history. Who knows where this'll go, but for now I feel very lucky."

"And so does he, I'm sure."

Hugh began to feel uneasy about conducting such an intimate conversation out on a public street corner.

"We do make an awkward trio, though" continued Anibel with a smile.

"Always have," said Hugh.

"With you wearing the collar and all."

"Look, no more needs to be said on the topic," said Hugh as nicely as he could. "I'm happy for you both. I hope it works out. I really hope it works out."

"Thank you," Anibel said with a note of finality in her voice. She kissed Hugh lightly on the cheek. Then she walked on to the museum and Hugh crossed the Green to the rectory, each pretending that the ground under their feet hadn't just shifted.

◆ ◆ ◆

As Danny Gill walked into the newsroom he did indeed feel like he was riding high, as Anibel had told Hugh. Here, amid the ringing phones, clacking typewriters and pounding wire machines, he was the man of the moment, the reporter with the big story and the promise of more to come. He'd noticed a change in the way the other reporters and editors spoke to him. There was a respect and maybe even a little envy detectable in their usual stream of profanity and cynical disparagement. He'd gotten friendly nods from ad sales reps, a few of the younger guys from the business side and, to his lasting pride and pleasure, a couple of typesetters he'd walked past in the parking lot. And now as he walked across the big noisy room it seemed as if every eye was upon him. Then he realized that every eye *was* upon him, and that a circle of editors and reporters had formed around his desk where, at their very center, another tube-shaped parcel wrapped in brown paper was awaiting his attention.

It was later, after the package had been carefully opened, the Monet haystacks unfurled and admired, the police called, Anibel and Hugh briefly informed, coffee poured, and his first sheet of copy paper rolled into place in his typewriter, that Dan took a moment to express an inner gratitude for, first of all, a huge story that now seemed to be writing itself, and, secondly, for a feeling of excitement in front of a keyboard that he hadn't felt since his salad days in Italy.

Right from the beginning, Dan's war had been very different from Hugh's—more glamorous and certainly less brutal. Somewhere down the long line of Gill connections an important string had been pulled and, following basic training, he was shipped to London with the idea that he'd do his war service as a correspondent for *Stars and Stripes*, the daily newspaper of the U.S. armed forces overseas. It was something he was interested in already, having been the energetic, sodbusting editor of the *Crosby Call*, but now he was headed for a crash course in newspapering—and living dangerously—that no standard hometown daily or college journalism course could ever touch.

He first spent a couple of months in *Stars and Stripes*' flagship London operation, where he performed mostly low-on-the-totem-pole tasks in a swirling hive of editors, reporters, military men, femmes fatales, mysterious polyglot strangers, and an endless stream of dispatches from battlefields all across the European Theater. He learned as he went, first by observing and then, because it was necessary, by doing. He loved London but knew he wouldn't be staying long. At the time, the main Allied front was located in Northern Africa, pressing eastward along the Mediterranean's southern rim toward Italy. When Dan was deemed ready by his reliably good work, potential for growth, and sturdy, independent nature, he was sent to Algiers to help out on the edition of *Stars and Stripes* published there.

After that, he was basically on his own, filling in for a correspondent who'd been wounded on the job. Dan moved with the American soldiers wherever they went. He'd spend time with them at the front, gathering news and jotting down the details of life there, and then he'd fall back to bang out copy on his trusty Remington portable and get the dispatch back to wherever the home base was at the time. One thing he learned along the way was that *Stars and Stripes* was for and about the soldiers in the war, not the brass and certainly not the politicians back home. Many of Dan's new colleagues were already seasoned professional journalists, and he fed off their dedication and no-bullshit adherence to the facts. He even got to rub shoulders with stars like Ernie Pyle and Bill Mauldin, both revered in every foxhole and desert oasis from Casablanca to Cairo. As the weeks and months went by, he saw the best and worst of men in combat. He heard grown men in agony call for their mothers, but he also understood for the first time how intoxicating danger could be.

By the late spring of 1944, while Hugh was training in New Guinea and the Philippines, Dan—still too young to get a legal drink back home—could sometimes be seen rattling around in a borrowed Jeep, armed with a Springfield rifle and a .25 caliber Italian automatic, an unlit cigar clenched in his teeth. With the Germans facing a major new front following the invasion of Normandy, they were now, following the siege at Anzio, backtracking up Italy's long boot. For a while, *Stars and Stripes* was able to set up shop in Palermo, where the issues were put together and printed, and then distributed via everything from C-47s to muleback. Then Rome fell. The newspaper staff, including Danny, got there before most of the troops did. They seized the press at *Il Messeggero* and saw to it that a paper with the headline "WE'RE IN ROME" was in soldiers' hands as they streamed into the city.

After that glorious moment, Italy gradually became what the soldiers there called "the forgotten front." The Germans resisted for almost another year further up north, but with its stable headquarters now located in Rome, the day-to-day at *Stars and Stripes* felt a little more routine. Dan continued to deliver news and even, to great acclaim, poetry of a sort to the paper's "Puptent Poets" feature—a memorable stanza that began, "Dirty Gertie from Bizerte/Hid a mousetrap up her skirtie." While looking for wartime color to write about, he also wandered the hill towns of Tuscany just short of the front lines. In Siena, he saw with a sudden aching for home the campanile that was the model for the train tower in Waterbury. In another place on the way to Pisa—he remembered it as San Miniato—he strolled at dusk with a local priest who spoke softly about the carillonneur's art and how his bells gave a sense of community, continuity and hope to the people in his town, even during the darkest days.

He stayed through the surrender of the Nazis' Army Group C in the first week of May 1945, and then the full German surrender five days later. He thought he'd then get sent to the Pacific, but with so many troops remaining behind, there was still a need for the newspaper, somewhat reduced in scope, so Dan stayed put. Rome hadn't been terribly damaged during the fighting, and it soon re-emerged as its immortal self, a sunny, open-handed, sensuous place for winding down and enjoying a lingering Italian autumn, which any war-weary 20-year-old was entitled to do.

◆ ◆ ◆

All of which served to explain, at least in part, Dan's boredom as he was faced with the relatively placid run of events back home. He wasn't one for seeking predictable routines as Hugh was. He'd come to the Waterbury paper from Woonsocket as the new cops and fires reporter, having decided early on that there was at least some chance for excitement on that beat, and that his stories about crime and misfortune would be high on the list of those that people actually read. The brazen art theft and its unsolved companion murders were like gold to him. Nothing would ever stir his blood like the war had, but now, 10 years on, he thought he detected a potentially thrilling echo. And to top it off, unexpectedly, honestly beyond all his hopes, there was Anibel, too.

So, yes, riding pretty high at day's end as he let himself into his apartment, a furnished first-floor one-bedroom on Holmes Avenue, just off the Green's west end. As soon as he stepped inside he heard a noise, a thump, maybe a footfall, and knew he wasn't alone. There was just daylight enough for him not to need to turn on a light. He grabbed a heavy, flask-shaped vase from the front-hall table and advanced several steps.

"Who's here?" he said.

His voice was forceful but there was no reply. He thought

he detected the slightest creaking of a floorboard and then a car went noisily up the street.

"Who's there?" he said again. "I'm coming in."

There was a sudden rush up the front steps behind him and then the door, which he hadn't quite closed, swung wide open and Anibel burst in, carrying an umbrella and an overnight case.

"What the hell are you doing?" she asked loudly as Dan, vase raised in his hand, turned toward her.

The visitor, who'd been in the darkened kitchen, made a dash out the side door, which was no doubt how he'd gained entry. Dan gave chase but by the time he got outside he couldn't tell which way to turn in the warren of garages, clotheslines, garbage cans and backyard fences. When he got back, Anibel was standing in the kitchen. She'd turned on the lights.

"What was that?" she asked.

"I don't know," said Dan, his adrenaline flowing.

"An intruder?"

"Yes."

"Waiting for you?"

"Yes, apparently."

"Tied into the story?"

"Has to be."

"Dan, is this yours?"

She was pointing to the wooden kitchen chair beside them, where a blackjack rested on the seat.

"No."

"Well then, you're part of the story now. I think we better call the police."

CHAPTER 7

"At the lowest level you've got the bums, hoboes, tramps and derelicts. Some of them wander, some loiter. They can be drinkers, Sterno eaters or just lost in their heads. You'd have to classify them as nuisances, almost always harmless except to themselves and other bums. I've found a surprising number of them to be clever and funny. Very good at physical humor."

Detective Alvin Walker was seated at his desk in Waterbury police headquarters, going over his personal hierarchy of bad guys for the benefit of Anibel Moss. Following the police visit to Dan's apartment and preliminary questioning regarding the intruder, Anibel and Dan had been asked to come downtown to make a formal statement. There, they'd covered all the bases, including their own extracurricular interest in the Wheeler case, which Walker was in charge of pursuing on the police side. They'd all agreed that the break-in at Dan's had to be tied into his reporting on the art theft and that the weapon—the "sap," Walker called it—was meant to be used, probably on the back of Dan's head. Even so, there was a feeling shared by all three that the original crime might now be unraveling at the back end, especially with the return of two of the paintings, a move that Walker admitted had thrown him all the way back to square one. He'd recommended that Dan secure his doors and windows, but he also thought the break-in and aborted assault reeked of disorganization and incompetence. His guess was that there was disagreement, maybe even chaos, within the ranks. He also thought that the breakdown in leadership could make the situation even more dangerous rather than less so. Hugh's name was never mentioned.

At the end of their session, while Dan stepped out for a moment to catch up on some police blotter business at the front desk, Anibel wondered aloud about what sort of person might be responsible for such an act. Detective Walker, a good veteran cop well known to Dan, but also something of a character and a joke-teller at stags, asked if she'd ever considered all the different levels of criminality in the world.

"You're a museum person," he'd said to her. "You've studied all the centuries of art and history, all the various schools of painters, for instance, and good for you. But what do you know of the other side of the tracks—the classification of thugs, crooks, low lifes and losers?"

"Very little," she'd replied, suddenly fascinated. "Actually, nothing at all."

For Anibel, just being in the police station, so close to the lockups, behind the scenes, as it were, was a thrill. The worn desks, the hanging globe lights, the drab painted plaster walls, the casual display of service revolvers, the general air of crime and punishment—it was almost as if she'd been dropped into a forbidden place, one small step away from actually sharing a cell with a criminal. Walker had seen this and decided she'd be ripe for a tutorial.

"The next level after bums would include petty thieves, like shoplifters, purse snatchers and pickpockets," he said now, "and let's not forget the scam artists, mostly working over the telephone these days but still some old-fashioned door-to-door guys. Waterbury seems to breed scam artists like rabbits. And then you've got your prostitutes."

"Do we have many prostitutes here?" Anibel asked in all innocence.

"Only since Colonial days," said Walker.

"I guess I'm just sort of unaware. I tend to mind my own business when it comes to things like that."

"If you know where to look, you'll spot them. They make it their business to stand out."

Anibel had studied prostitution in a Sociology course at Smith, but now she felt there easily could be one being questioned in the office next door.

"Anyway, those are the usually nonviolent criminals," Walker continued. "There are others—petty burglars, for instance—but that's most of them. When you bring one of these small-time guys in, it's usually called a pinch rather than an arrest. Then you have the large category of organized crime."

"The Gambinos," said Anibel. She'd read about them in *Life*. She enjoyed the way the name rolled off her tongue.

"Yes, the Gambinos would be one of the New York families that also does business in Connecticut," said Walker with a smile. "Genovese is another, and then you've got Colombo down in New Haven and Patriarca out east toward Providence and Boston."

"And they can be violent."

"Very much so. That's who they are—gambling, extortion, racketeering, drug trafficking, murder. The whole laundry list."

"Are they here in Waterbury?"

"They're definitely around. There are a couple of restaurants they like. But more to the point, we also have what I like to call our "local mafia."

"What's that?"

"It's like an informal gang of local guys—hoods—who know each other, grew up in the same neighborhoods, and can and do occasionally work with each other. They're street wise and corrupt and they can be violent on occasion. They're the ones we really have to watch and concentrate on."

"It was one of them who was in Dan's apartment, wasn't it?"

"Seems likely," said Walker. "Judging by the way he ran and left his weapon behind he must be pretty far down on the organizational chart."

"And maybe they're the ones responsible for the whole thing?"

"At this point, I wouldn't be surprised. I'll admit that we've been looking outside Waterbury when we should have been looking in."

"Do they have leaders?"

"Sort of, but it's fluid. They go away every once in a while."

"Vacation?"

"Prison."

Anibel laughed a little self-consciously.

"Right now, there's a young guy named Robert Creasy who wants to be in control," Walker continued. "They call him 'Bobo.' We've been aware of him since he was 10 years old. He's been in reform school and jail a couple of times. Now he thinks he's ready to run the local rackets. He's a very dangerous case."

At that point, Dan came back into the room. It was almost time to take Anibel home and put an end to the long day—but not quite.

"Russo gave me a good lead for a story tomorrow," he said to Walker, referring to the desk sergeant.

"What's that?" Walker asked.

"He mentioned the string of break-ins at other houses in the Wheelers' neighborhood leading up to the art theft. I hadn't noticed that before. It seems important."

"Just because Russo thinks it's important doesn't mean it is," said Walker with some irritation. "The big houses have long histories of being burglary targets."

"Well, it seems like it might have some bearing on the case," said Dan. "He said the things taken included paintings and other framed things on the walls, almost like practice runs."

"Russo needs to shut his fucking mouth," Walker said and then apologized to Anibel. "Anyway, they were minor things, not worth much."

Dan let it all sink in, then continued on.

"I also heard something else out front, and not from Sgt. Russo," he said.

"You had a productive 10 minutes out there. Congratulations."

"Word is that the Frenchmen gave up another name today."

Walker swore again, this time without an apology.

"Who was it?" Anibel asked Dan.

"He didn't say," said Dan. "Detective, care to comment?"

Walker considered his options.

"Yes, that happened today," he said at last. "We are looking for the gentleman in question so I can't give you his name. He hasn't been arrested. He's a person of interest. Dan, I need a couple of days before a story appears."

Dan didn't respond directly.

"Off the record, Al, is it a name known to you?" he asked.

"Off the record, yes," said Walker.

"Another one of the city guys?"

"Still off the record?"

Dan nodded.

"Yeah, an associate of the others. You're going to give us some time on this, right? This only came down a few hours ago."

"Okay, but it sounds like they had quite a party at the Wheelers that night," said Dan. "Lots of people invited."

With that, he motioned to Anibel.

"Time for us to head out," he said. "You've seen enough backroom horse trading for one day."

"I love it," Anibel said. "It makes me realize what a good girl I've been. But I do need to know that we'll be safe when we get home."

"We'll be together tonight," Dan said with a quick glance at Walker. "My place."

"I'd say quite safe," the detective said. "They wanted to scare Dan, maybe rough him up a bit, and you got thrown into the bargain. Are you scared?"

"Yes," said Anibel.

"Then they were successful, even though they probably have no idea who you are. Just in case, we'll have a patrol on your street tonight."

"Thank you. I don't think it will keep Dan off the story, though," said Anibel, suddenly feeling invested in things.

"Well, that's up to him," said Walker. "It'll only get more dangerous if he persists. The real Mafia guys are smart enough not to go after reporters. They know they can't win that fight. But not so with the local guys. They're always trying to prove themselves to each other."

"That's good for Anibel to know. Thanks, Cal," said Dan a little angrily.

With that, they got up and left for home.

◆ ◆ ◆

As Anibel and Dan drove by the Immaculate on their way back from the police station, Hugh was steeling himself for the short dash through the rain from the church to the rectory. He'd had a long day, too, marked by all the things that can fill up a parish priest's calendar. There'd been a poorly attended morning mass, then breakfast, then the regular Wednesday meeting of all the priests, at which they could address problems, make suggestions, go over housekeeping issues and reveal the subject of their upcoming Sunday sermons, so as not to step on one another's toes —not that people were likely to attend more than one service.

Hugh enjoyed the Wednesday meetings, and the way each priest brought his own personal style to the table. John Shutt was the no-nonsense administrator, always aware of his parish's standing in the archbishop's office. Aloysius Logue was another native Waterburian, notoriously ham-handed on the altar, but bright and talkative, with an endless supply of personal anecdotes at his disposal. Edward Ferraro was quiet and pious, maybe a little unfriendly, with a reputation for giving out severe penances. Eugene Fox was the rookie on the team, fresh from the seminary, ready to take on any task, still trying to figure out his priestly role. Hugh wasn't sure how the others saw him, though. His war record was held in the highest esteem, but he was probably thought to be a bit of a free thinker. Anyway, good men, not a shiftless soul among them, and good housemates, too, if it came to that. Hugh hoped none of them would ever have to know about his present situation.

This Wednesday's meeting brought with it the extra planning needed for the Assumption, Monday's celebration of Mary's ascent into heaven and a Holy Day of Obligation, meaning the church would be busy and nearly full. Monsignor Shutt determined that because there would be obligatory masses on two days in a row, along with collections at each, the normal second collection on Sunday for the Archbishop's Relief Fund would be cancelled.

"Even Father Logue would agree that passing the basket three times in two days would exact an unnecessary burden," he said, looking down the table and eyeing the priest who was in charge of overseeing the parish finances. "Archbishop O'Brien will have to do without."

Following the meeting, which lasted nearly two hours, Hugh went for the mail, had lunch and then drove over to St. Mary's Hospital to make the rounds among the patients, offering comfort, prayer and even Last Rites, if needed. Before leaving, he'd checked the names on the "Critical List" supplied by the city's two hospitals and published in the newspaper every day, but he didn't see any familiar names. Even beyond his pastoral duties, he enjoyed his time spent in the hospital. There, priests, minsters and rabbis from parishes, congregations and temples from all across Waterbury circulated through the corridors, making it an opportunity to see each other, catch up, and engage in a little shop talk. Hugh especially enjoyed his give-and-take with the nurses, many of them nuns, a couple of them war veterans, and quite a few equipped with a mordant wit and no-nonsense edge —and an utter competence—that Hugh found stimulating. He certainly preferred their acerbic world view to that of the teaching nuns across the street at the parish grammar school, also St. Mary's. They might have been tough on the students, but in the presence of priests they were for the most part overly deferential, he thought, and tended to flock together like the pigeons on the Green. Their unquestioning, childlike devotion to Church or parish rules was a source of fascination to him.

After that, it was stop-offs at a couple of convalescent

homes, where parishioners were ensconced—Mr. Harrigan with a stroke, Mr. Vaill with crippling senility—a quick drop-in at an amateur-league baseball game, where several of his old Crosby teammates were defying their advancing years and still playing pretty well, and then finally back to the rectory for a pre-Cana session, where he ignored his own lack of experience to give a couple of lovesick kids advice on marriage, sex and living together successfully and devoutly under the watchful eye of Christ.

It was not until that evening, as darkness fell after dinner, that Hugh found himself back in the church with some spare moments for reflection. He sat in the third-row pew and enjoyed the towering silence of the nave. He smiled again at the sight, just hours ago, of his high school classmate valiantly legging out a triple. Then, almost immediately, his thoughts took the inevitable turn: the theft, the murders, Teddy Valuckas, Dan and Anibel. Again, he reviewed his role as an unwilling participant who had passed along the torch and was now a mere interested observer. The busy day he'd just experienced was proof that he'd returned fully to his priestly routines—and that didn't even include his work with the parish food pantry for the poor, or determining the religious-instruction curricula for the coming school year, or encouraging the collection of clothing, toys and bedding to be sent to still-recovering missions in the Philippines. He of course remained curious about any news or progress in the case, but he hadn't contacted Dan for some days. He wondered if the new relationship between Dan and Anibel was the reason for that. He was happy for them but didn't need to go out of his way to see them together. He certainly didn't want to lose their friendship, though. It was a complicated situation, no doubt worthy of better organized self-examination and prayer at some point. Somewhere in this rising tide of thoughts, he dozed off. When he woke up, he saw that it had gotten late and that the night man for the church and rectory, Pat Crimmins, had slipped out, probably thinking Hugh was deep in prayer and shouldn't be disturbed. It was Hugh, then, who extinguished the banks of votive candles, turned out all the lights but one, locked up, and made the short dash through the rain.

Pat greeted him as he came into the rectory's vestibule.

"Awful weather," he said. "Will it ever end?"

"It always has," said Hugh with a smile. He grabbed the latest issue of *Commonweal* off the front table. "I think I'll just head straight upstairs."

"Did you get the candles and lights, Father?" Pat asked.

"I did."

"And locked up?"

"Yes."

"Thank you. But before you go, Father, here's something for you. I found it leaning up against the back door when I came in just earlier."

He turned toward Hugh, holding out a package, something rolled up like a tube and wrapped in brown paper, with Hugh's name written in big block letters down the side.

CHAPTER 8

In Waterbury, especially in summer, it was easy to know when rain was on the way. The low-pressure systems usually came up from the south, pushing before them a change in the air. In Waterbury's case, that meant the air first wafted across Naugatuck, the bordering small city to the south, and home to the smokestacks of the U.S. Rubber Company and Naugatuck Chemical. If Waterbury's air smelled like an acrid chemical-and-rubber cocktail, it almost always meant rain.

On this day, Sunday, August 13, 1955, there was excitement in the air, too, for the rain, lots of it, was arriving in the form of Hurricane Connie, already responsible for a good deal of wind and water mayhem in North Carolina and Virginia. The big storm's vanguard outer bands of clouds were already swirling overhead as Hugh, Dan and Anibel—Dan's so-called "advisory team"—sat together inside a secluded gazebo in Library Park to go over the latest developments.

It had been two nights since Hugh opened the package addressed to him and spread out the canvas on the rectory's dining room table. It was "The Rehearsal" by Degas, a magnificent representation of the artist's long focus on ballet and ballerinas. As it lay before him, Hugh tried to take it in and appreciate it, to revel in his momentary ownership of it, but that wasn't possible. The overriding, very disturbing truth was that his special knowledge of the case had been found out or possibly had always been known. He was exposed. Someone out there—the criminals themselves, apparently—knew that he knew something, or worse, had witnessed something tied into the theft and murders.

Now they were making sure that he'd be indelibly drawn into the crime's increasingly messy center.

His first duty had been to go to Monsignor Shutt's upstairs study, where he'd closed the door and told the whole story of his involvement: the appearance of Teddy Valuckas on Holy Saturday, his non-confession and flight from the confessional booth, his not quite damning admissions out on Leavenworth Street, his death, and then Hugh's revealing all to Dan and Anibel. His superior, scowling from within a wreath of pipe smoke, took it all in.

"You should have come to me first thing," he said at length. "Your role, and any questions regarding it, were matters for the Church to deal with."

"He never actually confessed," said Hugh.

"That's why it was a matter for the Church. If he'd completed his confession, you wouldn't be able to tell anyone—not me, not your friends, not anyone. Now you've dragged us all into a place we don't want to go."

The monsignor tapped his pipe on the arm of his chair.

"We'll have to deal with all of that later, and I expect the consequences will be severe," he continued, "but right now we have other obligations."

The two men went downstairs together, where Hugh showed him the painting. They called the police, who came quickly, with Det. Walker trailing by about 15 minutes and bristling with questions. Hugh told the detective the same story he'd told Msgr. Shutt. Walker seemed flabbergasted when Hugh's connection to Dan and Anibel was made known.

"How could you not have gone to the police with the Valuckas lead?" Walker had asked.

"I didn't want to involve the Church in what was by all evidence a pretty lurid crime," Hugh said. "I saw my involvement as tangential."

"So you went to the newspaper instead."

"I thought that after doing that I could exit the story."

"You could be charged, you know. Withholding evidence."

"I guess I felt I didn't have anything conclusive."

"No disrespect intended, Father, but since when do you get to decide that?"

That's how it went. Walker took his notes, and the canvas, and finally left. Hugh called Dan, who'd already heard something was up. He told Hugh he'd have to write a story, probably reporting that police thought "it was possible" that the priest had heard or overheard something to do with the crime and now was being drawn in by the perpetrator. He felt obligated to keep secret Hugh's identity as his source regarding Valuckas. Meanwhile, the bigger story—the mystery surrounding the theft, the murders and the return of three of the paintings—remained just as potent as ever.

Now the three of them sat in the park gazebo as clouds raced and roiled in the southern sky. They'd been thoroughly exposed to the police and Hugh's Catholic hierarchy as a meddlesome, pain-in-the-ass trio. Hugh and Anibel would no doubt be far better off minding their own business and going back to their already busy lives. But the truth was that they'd felt violated—Anibel by the break-in at Dan's apartment, Hugh by the delivery of the painting—and were unable to let go. They were active participants. To step aside now—well, it just felt impossible.

"You don't have to keep this up if you don't want to," said Dan to Hugh as he'd arrived. "You're going to get yourself into real trouble."

"I already am in trouble, and there will be consequences," said Hugh. "But justice is a Christian value, too. I feel like there's something really sinister behind all this, and if I can help stop it, I should."

"Plus there are so many unsolvable mysteries in your line of work," teased Anibel, "it's probably refreshing to work on one that maybe isn't."

"I do like talking it over like this," Hugh admitted, ignoring Anibel's smile. "Maybe we'll come up with some things that'll help Dan get to the bottom of the whole thing. It's just that I can't afford to be *seen* doing it now, so let's get going."

"Okay then, I do have some news," Dan announced. "The

autopsy report is in on Valuckas, or let's say I finally got my hands on it. It turns out his heart did indeed cease to function, but the coroner found what appears to be the trace of an injection mark on his neck that somehow no one saw the first time around. They theorize that it could have been possible for someone to overdose him with poison, or maybe potassium chloride."

"But they don't know for sure?" asked Anibel.

"There are no traces of poison. Potassium chloride isn't technically a poison but in large doses it apparently causes heart dysfunction and then gets absorbed into the system fairly quickly. It vanishes without a trace."

"Someone should tell Alfred Hitchcock about that one," said Anibel.

"I'm sure someone has," said Hugh. "But now, if you don't mind, for the sake of speed, clarity and my own understanding of where we are, let's go over what we know at this point. I'll start at the beginning. A group of low-level thugs, a large group it seems, takes four paintings out of the Wheeler house while they're away."

"Presumably the chauffeur is involved as well," said Anibel.

"Yes, even though there's no indication of his having criminal intentions in the past," said Dan. "None I could find, anyway."

"They make their getaway, but not before disposing of Murphy," Hugh continued. "All goes well, but then Teddy Valuckas gets a conscience. He comes to confess to me but then takes off. Then he sees me on the street and starts to confess again. I tell him no. Two days later he's dead."

"Now it seems certain that he was murdered, which, with autopsy in hand, I will be writing about tonight for tomorrow's paper," said Dan.

The storm's first fitful breezes were swirling ominously through the trees over the gazebo.

"You know, when we were on Leavenworth Street that day, Teddy did tell me that he confessed to someone else, or that he planned to. I don't remember which," said Hugh.

"His wife?" said Anibel.

"There's nothing to indicate that happened," said Dan. "Maybe another priest at another church in town?"

"If he was going to do that, then why confess to me?" Hugh asked. "But maybe there was someone else he got talkative with —the wrong person, as it turned out—and that's what got him killed."

"Maybe," said Dan, "but still, why was the painting sent to you?"

"Yeah, I don't know," said Hugh.

"It could be that he told someone that he'd talked to you, someone we don't know about," said Dan. "Maybe he even exaggerated and said he confessed to you. That would turn you into a target. Anyway, it's a fact that someone out there, let's call him the mastermind, knows about your involvement, sent you the painting and probably wonders exactly how much you know."

"But I really don't know anything," Hugh said. "Valuckas never really told me a thing."

"They don't know that," said Dan. "To them, the confessional is nothing more than a place where people reveal their darkest secrets to you."

Another pause. The air coming up the valley from Naugatuck was getting thick.

"Moving on," said Anibel, "the police get off track for a while, thinking it's an outside or even international job, but then one of the hoods brags about it to his friends and they bring in two suspects and charge them. They're deemed to be flight risks and so are held without bail. They eventually give up another name, but it doesn't sound like the name of a kingpin."

"I'm thinking the thieves probably never met the actual kingpin and were never told who he was," said Dan. "As far as they knew, Murphy was running the show."

"Then who gave Valuckas the order to shoot Murphy?" Anibel asked.

"That's the $64,000 question," said Hugh, using a new term that was sweeping the nation, "and it died with him. Now the paintings are being returned and no one knows what to make of that. If you're just going to return what you stole, how was it ever worth all the effort and sweat and risk in the first place?"

"Not to mention the deaths," said Dan.

"What are they trying to prove?" asked Hugh. "That they could get away with it? That they did it for the thrill of it? That they had a grudge against the Wheelers?"

They sat in silence a long moment, then Anibel spoke.

"Speaking of whom, guess where I'm going tonight?"

"Where?" said Dan, who felt he should already know.

"Sunday supper at the Wheelers, at the very WASPy dot of six o'clock."

"Wow, moving up in society. Who else will be there?" asked Hugh.

"I didn't have the nerve to ask, but I'm hoping some potential donors to the museum—and I'm not talking about arrowheads and teacup collections."

"Be sure to turn the conversation around to the thefts," said Dan. "You never know what they might suddenly remember."

"I don't see how that can be avoided," said Anibel. "We're going to be surrounded by empty walls."

"And don't get caught in the storm," added Dan. "It's going to be ferocious."

"Welcome once again to the house of infamy," Alice Wheeler said with a smile as Anibel entered a little after 6. "Give your raincoat to Mary and come through for a cocktail."

Anibel passed her coat and umbrella along to the pretty young girl in attendance. She wondered for the first time what kind of toll Murphy's violent death had taken on those who'd worked alongside him in service. Had the staff been comfortable enough with the police to tell all they knew? It was something for Dan to consider if he hadn't already. He'd be able to have a cutie like Mary talking in no time.

"It seems we might not be getting the full brunt," Alice said over her shoulder as she led the way in, "but lots and lots of rain." She spoke with the deeply assured, nearly musical tones of the long-seated upper class, which Anibel had learned to identify while at Smith.

"Which we really don't need," she responded. She'd walked up the hill from her apartment on Linden Street. "The gutters are already gushing."

"And the river is rising!" boomed a male voice from up ahead. "Man the lifeboats!"

Anibel and Alice now entered a richly wood-paneled salon of sorts with a built-in bar at one end. Three men and a woman stood by the bar, drinks already in hand, now turning to consider the new addition. Anibel felt comfortable and confident, although maybe just a little bit windswept, in her red and black bolero suit—the pleated skirt and bolero red, the light sleeveless sweater black. She was happy to see she'd neither over- nor under-dressed. She handed Alice Wheeler a small wrapped hostess gift from the museum's shop. She felt ready for a martini.

The others in the room were Seth Wheeler, of course, who'd made the welcoming "lifeboat" cry, Dick and Doris Minor, a prominent older local couple with solid cultural credentials, and the third man, introduced as Pierre Henri, visiting from Paris.

"Pierre is an art dealer and scholar with a specialty in the Impressionists," said Seth. "He's helped us with our decisions for years and now he's come to help us sort out our collection and our future moves in the wake of the incident. Luckily for us, he speaks English very well."

As the group continued its small talk about the weather, Anibel sipped her martini and glanced around the room. This is where the stolen paintings had hung and where the Whistler still did, basking in its new solitary status. The room's faded walls hadn't been re-papered in many years, and now the empty rectangles where the Monets, Manet and Degas had hung stood out in sharp relief, almost as a kind of modern "statement" art, Anibel thought. She wondered if the Wheelers would refurbish the walls and re-hang the paintings or just move away.

The expert from France was now holding court with a story of an especially rough ocean crossing. He was a small man with dark, tufty eyebrows and a continental, Claude Rains sort of air. He turned to Anibel as he came to the end of his story and wondered if she, as the youngest in the group, had ever considered traveling to Europe by boat or if that mode of travel had now become a thing of the past.

"I think the war, and Korea, too, have taken the romance out of travel for now, at least for people of my generation," Anibel said. "Too many dead in the oceans and falling from the sky, and even just too many difficult passages and experiences abroad. Bad associations. Home feels better for now."

"Understood, but surely it will come back at some point," said Dick Minor.

"Yes, but I think probably by air," said Anibel. "Speed will be the thing, won't it?"

"Again, the influence of the war—so many things moving so fast," said Alice.

"Or maybe space travel will be next," said Dick with a laugh. "They say it's right around the corner."

"Not much romance up there, I'm afraid," said Alice.

"Imagine, stripping the moon of its mystery," Henri said wistfully. "That must not be allowed."

"If it is, what will songwriters ever rhyme with 'June'?" said Seth, draining his drink and placing his glass on the bar. "I see by Alice's nod that it's time to take our seats for dinner."

The meal was good, uncomplicated fare prepared and promptly served by Mrs. Watkins, the Wheelers' longtime cook. Fruit cocktail was followed by cream of celery soup, then a lime sherbet palate cleanser, then beef Stroganoff, and finally a lemon meringue pie that Doris Minor had brought in with her from Woodbury. The wine was a fine Bordeaux from the Wheelers' extensive cellar, warmly commended by the visiting Frenchman. The topics of conversation ranged widely from interplanetary space travel to the films of Fred Astaire and Ginger Rogers to the lasting architectural legacy of downtown Waterbury, before settling at long last, over pie and coffee, on the subject so very much at hand.

"It's kind of a miracle that the paintings are being returned," Dick Minor said to Seth. "When do you hope to get them back on your walls?"

"No idea. They tell me they have them in a special safe in the police evidence room," Seth said. "I certainly hope so. It turns out we have them insured for about a tenth of their actual value."

"We've lived with them for so long, we had no real idea," added Alice a little defensively.

All eyes turned to Henri.

"They are certainly galloping along in value," he said. "A good Cezanne might get over $100,000 at auction now, with Renoir not far behind. Your Monet, Manet and Degas are rising rapidly, too."

"How hard would they be to move on the black market?" Anibel asked.

"Not hard at all. The art world is still very fluid in Europe right now. Borders and jurisdictions remain a little uncertain. It's a good time to unload stolen goods."

"But in this case that seems not to be the thief's goal," said Dick.

"No," said Henri. "Unfortunately, or should I say fortunately, the workings of the criminal mind are not known to me. Returning the paintings—like the rest of you, I can only wonder at it."

Seth Wheeler produced a tray crowded with an assortment of after-dinner drinks. As he took orders, he spoke.

"I think of my father as such a young man, making the rounds in Paris," he said. "He had such a well-developed sense of what he wanted to buy—and an unlimited wallet thanks to my grandfather—but I wonder if he bought what he liked or what he thought would eventually bring the most return."

"Surely it was what he enjoyed and admired," said Henri.

"From an aesthetic viewpoint, he chose only the best. Otherwise, why not go ahead and purchase real estate or stocks?"

"My grandfather made those investments, too," said Wheeler. "But he'd been burned in the Panic of 1873 and what they called the Long Depression that followed. He apparently never fully trusted the safety of the conventional marketplace again."

"Well, somehow between your grandfather's money and your father's choices, they made some very wise decisions," said Anibel.

"Seth's dad was always willing to trade his artworks up, down and sideways," said Alice. "He bought and sold over a thousand in his lifetime. Even Whistler's "White Girl" went when its time came. But never the ones that hung here and in the other room. He had real affection for them."

"They'd actually been placed by my grandfather when he built the house in 1895," explained Seth. "They've always felt kind of sacrosanct to me, a part of the house and the family tradition."

"You poor dears," said Doris Minor. "You must have such confused feelings right now. Sell, store, put back on the wall, distribute to your kids, send off to museums—which is the correct course?"

"That's why we have Henri here to help us decide," said Alice. "We'll sit down tomorrow and begin."

"First, though, when we say our prayers tonight, we will thank God for the returned paintings," said Henri.

"While hoping the last one is on its way, too," said Alice.

"And praying, too, that the sick human being, or beings, behind this whole thing can be found out and brought to some form of rough justice," said Seth.

After a moment, Anibel spoke. She saw clearly that the Wheelers were compelled to go over and over the details of the theft with friends and each other, hoping that some previously overlooked thought might be dislodged and lead them to an answer. She thought Dan was doing the same thing, and Hugh, and the police. It had become a general obsession. Now she wanted to pursue a line of thought as well.

"I'm sure you've gone over this ad nauseum with the police," she said to the Wheelers, "but what are your personal feelings about Thomas Murphy's role in the theft?"

"There's still lots of room for not knowing his full role," said Seth. "The police say he was involved in that he gave the orders to the lower-downs in the operation, the ones who are now in jail. He let them in, he pointed out the paintings to be taken, and then he left with them, either voluntarily or not, either alive or not. But who was giving him his orders, and under what circumstances, we don't know."

"To us, he was a good man," said Alice. "He'd come with excellent references from right here in the neighborhood, had been with us for five years, lived over the garage, never a complaint or a problem."

"And then they murdered him for his trouble," said Dick Minor.

"I often wonder if he questioned why they were taking the rug from the entrance hall as they left, the one they wrapped him up in. He wouldn't have seen that as part of the plan," said Alice. "Or maybe he was already bound and gagged and knew he was done for. Or maybe he was already dead."

"He died with many secrets, obviously," said Seth. "But the main one for me is who put him up to this, and why, and why couldn't he—Murphy—have come to us or the police about it?"

The conversation then trailed off until the coffee urn was empty and it was time to go home. The rain continued to pour and the wind had grown strong enough to cause the Wheelers' lights to flicker two or three times during dessert. Mrs. Watkins said a radio bulletin warned about flooded city streets and downed branches and power lines. The Minors offered to give Anibel a ride home, which she gladly accepted. As they drove down the hill, she already regretted the double pour of Grand Marnier. When she got back to her apartment, she changed quickly into her nightgown and got into bed. She listened to the rain sweep through the tree limbs and wondered what she'd learned, if anything, at the Wheelers. Seth and Alice were still reeling, obviously. The little man from Paris was an interesting unknown—erudite, outwardly friendly but self-absorbed, and she thought a little untrustworthy around the eyes. Probably nothing newsworthy for Dan, though. No new ideas about the return of the paintings, or about Murphy's true role. Murphy remained an enigma. There's nothing more unknowable than a dead bachelor, Anibel thought as she drifted off, unless, of course, it's a live priest.

◆ ◆ ◆

Hugh was working late, tinkering with his Monday sermon, as the storm raged. He felt secure in the sturdy rectory, even with rainwater beginning to pool out on West Main Street. He liked to be topical in his sermons, citing headlines or modern ethical dilemmas rather than falling back on the classic old lessons from the gospels. He knew that the art theft and murders had lately influenced his choices, although he never mentioned them specifically. He'd preached on the theft of property vs. the theft of life, and the unchanging place of God in an increasingly violent, everchanging society. Now he was working on the idea of the confessional as a two-way street, ideally consisting of a conversation rather than just a confession and a penalty. His head was bowed over his yellow legal pad when he was startled by the ringing of the rectory's front-door bell. He heard the door creak open and a brief conversation that wasn't quite audible. Then he heard Pat Crimmins trudging up the stairs and stopping in front of his door. Then a knock. Hugh stood and stretched. He had every reason to dread an unexpected nighttime caller.

"Yes, Pat," he said to Crimmins as he opened the door.

"I'm sorry to bother you, Father, but there's a visitor downstairs who wants to see you. I tried to put him off, but he insisted."

"Okay, Pat, thanks. I'll go down."

Hugh walked down the broad front stairs. The entrance hall below was only dimly lit by a small lamp on a side table. At first, he didn't see anyone, but then he made out a dark figure in a corner. He thought it might just be a poor congregant seeking shelter for the night.

"Good evening," said Hugh. "What can I do for you?"

The figure moved toward him. As he did, Hugh could see he was wearing a trench coat, thoroughly drenched, and a fedora pulled down low across his brow. Then he tilted his head upward and made himself known, looking Hugh straight in the eye.

"I'd like you to baptize me," said Sandy Jones.

CHAPTER 9

With an uncomfortable feeling, Hugh led Jones into the library and closed the door behind them. He took his dripping coat and spread it out over the back of a chair and hung his hat on a convenient peg. They took seats facing each other in a pair of well-used green leather armchairs. Jones was pasty-faced, save little washed-out smudges of light pink on his cheekbones. He exuded an acrid stench of tobacco and whisky so strong that Hugh could taste it in his throat.

"Can I get you anything, Sandy? Coffee or water?"

Jones waved off the offer.

"Well, why don't you tell me what this is all about," Hugh said.

"I've already told you, Hugh old chum. I want you to baptize me."

He was trying hard to be airy and casual in an old-boy sort of way—absurd under the circumstances—but his appearance spoke of nothing less than panic.

"That's an unusual request to make on the spur of the moment in the middle of the night," Hugh said.

"Is there a rule against it?"

"Technically, no," said Hugh. "But the longstanding practice for adults wishing to be baptized has been to establish a period of time for study and reflection."

"Do you suppose that's what John the Baptist did—told people to come back later?"

"No, probably not," Hugh admitted.

Jones leaned forward in his chair, his elbows on his knees,

his hands clasped together.

"Look, I got you into my club without the usual rigamarole. Now I want you to do the same for me."

"The Catholic Church isn't a club, Sandy."

"Isn't it? You've got rules, rituals, costumes, secrets, dues. People say they *belong* to a church the same way they talk about belonging to a club."

"Don't you already belong to a church?"

"Yes, for a long time at St. John's. For a lifetime. But the Episcopalians don't offer the one thing I need and that I can get from you."

"And what's that?"

"Ironclad confession and forgiveness. Open and shut. No room for argument or equivocation."

Hugh stood and walked over to where Jones' raincoat was drying. He made a slight adjustment to it, centering the shoulders more precisely on the chairback.

"What are you afraid of, Sandy?" he asked after a moment.

Jones looked up at him. He was hollow-eyed and shaken, no longer the domineering heel feared by all in the grill room. Any bravado he'd come in with was short-lived, probably booze-fueled, and now abandoning him.

"I've just been roughed up pretty well, Hugh," he said, shifting to a softer tone. "I've just come from it. Struck in the midsection so the marks don't show. I've had demands made that I can't meet, and more violence will follow."

Whatever Hugh had been expecting, this wasn't it. This was nighttime Jones, the side of him that others talked about behind his back—something sick and dangerous and often leaving a trail of consequences. Might there be drugs in the mix, or illicit sex, or gambling debts? With Jones it could be any of those things. And now, like a shifty creature of the dark, he'd been drawn to the one light he thought was obliged to offer refuge.

"You need to go to the police," Hugh said.

"I can't possibly. I have a history with the police in this town that you don't know about. You know a lot, more than I would have guessed, but you don't know that."

Hugh wasn't sure what Jones was driving at. He came back and sat down again.

"You know, when you left the club it hurt me a great deal," Jones said. "I took it very personally. I'd gone to great lengths to bring you in."

That would be something for another day, Hugh decided. He saw that Jones was becoming unsteady, maybe close to passing out.

"Who are the people making demands on you, and what is it that they need from you?" Hugh asked.

"I can't go there," Jones said. "Not like this. That's why I asked for baptism. I have to change the ground rules."

"Alright, I see," said Hugh. There was a lack of empathy in his voice that he hoped Jones was too drunk to notice. "We obviously can't do it tonight and it's a very busy weekend with a holy day on Monday. You don't want to be baptized in front of the whole congregation, I take it."

"Not on your life."

"Then we might have to wait a few days. That'll also give you time to calm down and decide if this is really what you want to do. Believe me, this arrangement would still be far quicker than normal church procedure."

Jones wasn't happy, but he accepted Hugh's terms with an assenting grunt. For his part, Hugh wasn't at all sure about what he'd do. He was buying time. He'd be willing to listen to Jones' cascading list of sins and transgressions if it came to that, but he was more bothered right now that the man had been beaten up and was possibly being blackmailed. What awful line had Jones crossed? What sort of help might he need beyond whatever baptism offered? His eyes were closed now. His breathing was rough but regular. Hugh looked at him for a long moment—the touches of rouge, the dyed black hair, the waste of it all—before getting him standing and back into his hat and coat. He called for a cab. He told Jones he'd phone him on Tuesday or Wednesday and sent him back out into the night.

As he climbed back up the stairs onto the rectory's quiet second floor, Hugh decided there was a lot he didn't like at all about Jones barging in like that, wanting to convert. Certainly, there was an air of desperation to it. Worse, Hugh felt that Jones had come to him, personally, rather than to the Church as a whole. But maybe that was the best the man could do. Hugh could be guilty of always trying to see the best in situations. Was Jones truly seeking redemption? Maybe. Could he genuinely be sorry for his sins? And what, exactly, were his sins? Hugh wasn't in a position to know. Still, the whole thing had an air of unreality to it. It was yet another unforeseen consequence of his selfishly taking the golf membership. Could Sandy Jones actually soon become a parishioner at Hugh's own Immaculate Conception? That'd put a real sinner and black sheep in their midst if only half the stories about him were true.

Following the celebration of mass for the Feast of the Assumption the next morning, and Hugh's brief but well received sermon on confession, he got on the phone with both Dan and Anibel, asking what they knew, if anything, about Sandy Jones. He didn't say much about why he was asking. He wasn't quite sure himself. He knew about Jones from his personal dealings with him, mostly at the club and mostly unpleasant. To Dan and Anibel, he mentioned only that Jones was showing an interest in converting. He wondered if they knew of any serious red flags he should be aware of. Dan told him he'd always thought of Jones as a classic WASP failure and an unsavory character, possibly worse than that, and that when he got the chance, he'd check with his police sources and go through Jones' folder in the newspaper's morgue of clippings. Anibel was more forthright. She said straight out that she'd be astounded if Jones ever converted to Catholicism.

"Why do you say that?" Hugh asked.

"You don't know about the Joneses versus the Church? Your church?"

"I don't think so."

"It's a great Waterbury story," she said. "I'm surprised you've never heard it."

Then she told the tale of when the Immaculate Conception parish was looking for larger quarters in the mid-1920s, having concluded that the old church on East Main Street was too small to absorb the waves of expanding Catholic families and new faces coming to the city to work at the factories. The hierarchy by that time had grown ambitious. It felt it was time for Catholics to assert themselves by joining their Congregational and Episcopalian brethren right at the center of Waterbury, on the Green. They surveyed the possibilities and found the most likely parcel was the Jones property, at the foot of Prospect Street. The house and land were available, but there was a problem. The Joneses were dyed-in-the-wool, Pope-detesting Protestants and would never sell to the Catholics.

What happened next has always been a bit unclear, Anibel continued. With the help of several sympathetic city officials and a handful of others—some of whom perhaps had reason not to like Sandy Jones—an elaborate ruse was put into motion and, long story short, the Joneses ended up selling their property in 1925 to a Church-backed straw man named Mortimer King. Within weeks, the old Jones homestead was knocked flat and construction of the grand new church and rectory was under way.

Sandy Jones, who as a young lawyer at the time was in charge of his family's interests, had been royally hoodwinked. It was said that he seethed with anger and spoke ill of the Church at every opportunity. But the capper came a few years later, in 1928, when the enormous new church was to be officially dedicated. Sandy had by then moved to a house up the hill on Prospect Street. It was a gorgeous Sunday morning in May and a big golf day for him, but the crowds for the dedication were such that cars lined both sides of Prospect Street, including, it seemed, right across the front of his driveway. He couldn't get out. His anger at the Catholics now reached a new level. He first called the rectory, but of course everyone was in the church, attending the dedication mass. He next tried the archdiocese office in Hartford, but the archbishop was also co-officiating at the ceremony in Waterbury. It's said that Sandy Jones next telephoned Rome, demanding to speak directly with the Pope. Needless to say, he never got through, and his hatred of the Church has only doubled and redoubled ever since.

"I don't see how it's possible that he now wants to become a Catholic," Anibel concluded. "We can laugh at the story, but it's a deadly serious thing with him. His defining episode, maybe. He's the one who shamed the family name by being so easily bested by what they all thought of as the inferior beings, mostly Irish, associated with the Church. I was told the story by an old-line museum board member who knew Jones well. He said he was never the same afterward, even that he'd been ruined by it."

Hugh thanked Anibel for the story, and the perspective on Jones.

"I wondered at the time why he picked you out to have a membership at the country club," Anibel said. "Why he'd want a Catholic priest there at all."

"I guess I didn't give that much thought. I figured very egotistically that I was the only priest in the city who was good enough to play with him and have a drink and act sociably over a game of cards. I was flattered to the point of blindness."

"Well, you must have done a good job. Now he wants to join your team."

"Does he though, Anibel? I think he might just be terribly confused."

"Was he drunk?"

"Yes."

"I bet he was. Listen, Hugh, I have my own theory about all this."

"What's that?"

"Sandy Jones has a crush on you."

"Really?" said Hugh. The possibility hadn't occurred to

him. "Does he like men?"

"I don't know who he likes. I think probably his compass is all over the place when it comes to those sorts of things. Anyway, I don't necessarily mean a romantic crush. Maybe he's just drawn to you because you're so cute and unavailable. Some people get their kicks that way. I've known the feeling myself."

Hugh missed the reference.

"Well, I think it's possible that he just wants to go to heaven," he said. "He thinks I'm the one who can help him get there."

"That's why you're Glass-Half-Full Hugh. I have to go now, but based on the few things I've heard, I'd be careful about where this might lead."

◆ ◆ ◆

Dan didn't call until late in the afternoon on Monday, but he was full of news when he did.

"They brought in the third guy last night," he said to Hugh. "A local punk named Mars who'd been hiding out with family in New Jersey."

"Where does that leave us?" asked Hugh.

"Well, nothing official, but Walker, the detective, told me all the arrows are pointing in the same direction now, in instead of out, and most likely to a guy who thinks of himself as a local boss."

"Who's that?"

"Name of Creasy. Maybe you heard about him."

"I haven't."

"Walker says he mentioned him to Anibel. He's young and dangerous, maybe a little crazy. Thinks he'll live forever. He wants to be the local kingpin."

"Did they arrest him?"

"They're studying him real close, leaning on his friends, checking his habits, making sure his license plate is on straight and his taillights are working. They'll bring him in on something and see if they can proceed from there. Might take a few days."

"They think he's the one responsible?" asked Hugh.

"Yeah, I guess so."

"For the theft of Impressionist paintings from France?"

Dan sighed.

"What do you want from me? I'm just a reporter."

"And then out of the blue he starts sending them back again?"

Dan didn't answer. He saw problems with the theory, too. He switched the topic.

"While I was at the station, I asked about Sandy Jones," he said. "Walker sent me to a guy who does vice investigations, and he pretty much confirms what I told you before. Jones is a known character to them. A bad guy. Sick. He flits around in the dark corners of Waterbury, but they've never got him on anything serious. Just small stuff and lots of warnings."

"And friends in high places."

"Not as high as yours, Father," Dan said with a smile, "But, yeah, it probably doesn't hurt."

"Anything else?"

"This cop told me Jones likes 'em young and has a reputation for that. He didn't elaborate or say how young. But he's apparently all over the map with drinking and drugs and dirty pictures. Some gambling too. They're impressed with his stamina. He'll stop for a while when he gets into a jam, but then he always comes back in again. He has to have lost a fortune. At one point early on he apparently had two mistresses, each put up in a separate place and supplied with all the essentials."

"Great," said Hugh with a sigh. "He sounds like a perfect candidate for salvation. Did I tell you? He wants me to baptize him into the Church."

"Sounds like you're gonna need a lot of holy water," said Dan.

"Yeah, as I told Anibel, he wants to get into heaven, but he doesn't have to be a Catholic to do that. I don't have the secret code."

"You and your folks in Rome, you kind of intimate that you do."

"Well, I guess I'll have to sit down and have a long talk with him before we go any further. Thanks for your help, Dan. These are things they just don't teach you in the seminary."

◆ ◆ ◆

That evening, Dan called Hugh again and this time was nearly breathless with excitement.

"Hugh, you're not going to believe this one," he said. "You have to come meet me. Ten minutes in the library reading room. Can you do it?"

"I'll be there," said Hugh.

Waterbury's public library was a handsome three-story brownstone located in its own park on Grand Street, between Dan's office and Hugh's rectory. Hugh, walking fast, entered beneath the building's front porte-cochere. He saw Dan already seated at the end of one of the reading room's long wooden tables. In front of him was a manila envelope. He gave Hugh one of his ridiculously dashing smiles. Hugh sat down.

"After I spoke with you on the phone, I came back to the paper and got the librarian to pull Jones' file from the morgue," Dan said. "My interest was running high after everything the cops told me. His stuff isn't too extensive, though. Mostly golf championships and an occasional Society Page photo taken at a holiday dance or charity event. Nothing at all that would point to what we talked about earlier."

"But?" said Hugh.

"But."

Dan opened the envelope and pulled out a yellowing old clipping.

"Take a look at this."

Hugh took the article from Dan and held it up to the light.

It was a 1949 story about Jones' many conquests on the links. It recounted his championships won and his standing in the golfing community, both locally and nationally. It was accompanied by a large photo of him, posing with a golf club on what appeared to be his front lawn.

"This seems perfectly normal to me, Dan," Hugh said.

"Well, it's not," said Dan. "Take another look at it, closer. Look up on the porch behind him, standing in the shadows. Who do you see?"

Hugh did as he was told and saw the barely visible figure, half-hidden by a pillar, he'd missed the first time around. He stared at it and then the world around him spun just a little

"That's Thomas Murphy," Hugh said.

"There's no mistaking it," said Dan. "I must have looked at his photo a thousand times when he was missing. I'd know him anywhere."

"Even on Sandy's porch."

"Even in the shadows."

Hugh looked at it again. It was almost as if the dead man was trying to speak to him.

"What does it mean?" Hugh asked.

"I'm almost afraid to say," said Dan. "Could be nothing, could be something. Maybe we just follow it where it leads us."

"That sounds a little simplistic. Are you going to write about it?"

"I can't. There's nothing for me to say. I don't have any context for it that I can write about at this point."

Hugh took the leap.

"Could this somehow tie Jones to the art theft?"

"I don't know."

"The murders?"

"I don't know."

"Of course, we're probably prone to jumping to conclusions right now."

"Well, I doubt they were plotting out crimes together six years ago when the photo was taken."

"Maybe not," said Hugh, "but it does prove they knew each other and maybe even that Murphy worked for Jones."

"In all my reporting, no one has ever mentioned that," said Dan.

"Well, there's clearly some sort of relationship going on. Should we call up the police about it?"

Dan stood and slipped the clip back into its envelope.

"They're pretty busy right now," he said cagily. "Let's give them a break. We don't want to tire them out. They can read my story in the morning."

Those were the last words Dan was ever to say to Hugh. Late that night, after filing his report naming Mars and Creasy and thus pulling the knot a little tighter on the Wheeler case, Dan walked up State Street toward his apartment. Anibel wouldn't be waiting for him, as she sometimes did. She was at her own place. But on Friday, he remembered with pleasure, they had a date planned. The State Theater was hosting the world premiere of the movie "The Girl Rush," starring Waterbury native Rosalind Russell. What's more, Russell was to be there in person, accepting the accolades of her old hometown and no doubt a key to the city. Dan had loved Russell ever since her spectacular portrayal of fast-talking reporter Hildy Johnson in "His Girl Friday." He'd managed to grab tickets for the premiere through the newspaper. Not that they were trying to hide anything, but until now he and Anibel hadn't been seen out together, not officially, not with her on his arm. He was looking forward to it. He knew she was, too.

He was smiling as he bounced up the four steps at the front of his building on Holmes Avenue. He never saw the figure crouched in the shadows. No words were exchanged. The man sprang up and shot Dan four times at close range before he could reach the door. The assailant stood over him briefly and then ran down the steps and up the street. Neighbors heard the shots and called the police. Dan was still breathing when the ambulance arrived, but he died during the ride to the hospital.

CHAPTER 10

It was Dan's father, Dr. Gill, who came to tell Hugh, ringing the rectory bell to deliver the news in person. Hugh came downstairs in his bathrobe. It was well after 1 a.m. When he saw Dan's dad standing in the entry hall, looking up at him, a dazed look on his face, he knew something terrible had happened. Hugh walked over to him, extending a hand, but the older man pulled him in firmly and close, with affection, as he would with a son of his own. Hugh could see he'd been crying.

"We've lost Danny," he said.

Hugh felt his insides weaken.

"He was murdered tonight on his own doorstep," Dr. Gill continued. "Coming home from work. Never made it to the hospital alive. They shot him, Hugh—shot *Danny*!"

He was incredulous, in shock, perhaps not quite fully comprehending. He looked at Hugh as if he wanted him to say that, no, he was mistaken, and that Danny was fine, that he was just up the stairs, listening to the radio. For a long moment they stood clasping each other's shoulders as if they might otherwise fall. Hugh earlier had heard the sirens going back and forth as he'd read in bed. He was having trouble taking it in. He knew there was some considerable danger in what Dan was reporting, but never this.

"Do the police have who did it?" he finally managed.

"No."

"I just saw Dan tonight."

The words were just words with no meaning.

"It's this story he's been working on, isn't it?" Dr. Gill asked, struggling to regain his composure. "This wasn't just a robbery or something."

"I think it must be," said Hugh. "He's been getting closer to those responsible. I think he was in the process of naming someone he hadn't named before."

Even though Hugh had trained himself as part of his job to remain stoic and dependable and even uplifting in the face of suffering and death, and had done so many times in the past, he now broke down. Dan was gone. His other half. All those years together, everything they'd done, erased by an act of evil and stupidity, one that he could see would leave Dan's father—this wonderful, generous, optimistic man—forever marked by sadness.

Hugh gathered himself and took a deep breath.

"How is Mrs. Gill?" he asked.

"Terribly stricken," her husband said. "Her daughters have come to be with her. I've got to get back to them. I've just come from the hospital. I had to identify Dan's—"

He wasn't able to finish the sentence.

"I'll come up and see her in the morning," Hugh said. "You should get back up to the house and try to get some sleep. Please allow me to give you a blessing."

"Before you do that, Hugh, do you know anything that might help find the murderer?"

"I might," said Hugh.

"It's no time for holding back."

"I understand. I will call the police as soon as you've gone, but I'm quite sure they already have a good idea of who did it."

"Who?"

"Based on what Dan told me today, I think it's the head of the local gang that stole the Wheelers' paintings. The police were closing in on him and so was Dan."

"Who is it?"

"A wild man named Creasy. I'm sure his name will show up in the story Dan wrote tonight."

"I have to go tell the police," said Dr. Gill.

"They already know. They were already going after him."

"I have to make sure."

"Why don't you stop at the crime scene on your way home. I'm sure there'll still be a detective or a patrol there. You can tell them."

Another long silence. The hallway clock chimed two.

"Alright, Hugh. I didn't know whether to wake you or wait until morning, but I thought you'd want to know."

"Of course. You did the right thing. We're going to have to learn to deal with this, and lean on each other when we have to, and hope that justice is swift."

"Justice won't bring my boy back, Hugh."

"No."

"And neither will prayers."

"No, but maybe they can help us cope," said Hugh. "Sometimes it helps if you think someone is listening and you say what you need to say. Now allow me to bless you and let you go."

He made the Sign of the Cross over Dr. Gill's forehead.

"May the grace and peace of Christ be with you," he said.

"And also with you," Dan's father responded.

As he was about to go back out the front door, Dr. Gill turned once again to Hugh.

"We understand that Dan and Anibel Moss have been seeing quite a bit of each other lately and that it might have been leading to something," he said. "We think it might be best if you were the one to tell her."

"Yes, I'll do that," said Hugh. He'd already thought of Anibel. "I think I'll let her have a peaceful night of sleep, though. She won't have another one for a very long time."

Before he went back up to his room, Hugh made two phone calls. One was to the newspaper, where he reached a graveyard-shift editor who assured him that Dan's story would run in the morning, along with the account of his murder. An obituary would follow a day or two later. He added that the details in Dan's story had already been conveyed to the police so they wouldn't have to wait until morning to see them. Hugh's next call was to police headquarters, where he tracked down a detective on duty who assured him they were fully aware of Creasy and his possible role in the shooting.

◆ ◆ ◆

Hugh decided to phone Anibel at 6 sharp. He knew he had to be straightforward with her, the same way Dr. Gill had been with him. He agonized as the sweep hand on his watch made its final turn. No amount of prayer and preparation could get him ready for a moment like this. She picked up on the second ring. Hugh told her that he had very bad news for her, the worst possible news. He said Dan had been shot and killed on his front porch. He added that he'd died immediately and had suffered no pain, something his wartime experiences had taught him to say. He felt like he could have spoken for an hour into Anibel's shocked silence. He could hear that she was sobbing. He didn't want her to be alone. He told her that they should meet, if possible, in a half-hour on a park bench across the street from his church's front steps. She said softly that, yes, she'd be there.

Hugh went out right away to wait for her. He'd been awake since Dan's father left. He'd sat in a kind of fog on the edge of his bed. The hours grew very long, but he had a whole life's worth of memories of Dan to go through. He'd always admired Dan's outgoing personality and easy charm. He recalled some of the places they'd gone together as teenagers where a word or two from Dan's silver tongue had smoothed the way into an event or party, or out of trouble. Hugh felt he should pray, but the loving consideration of Dan, the memories of their times together, was working better. He did pray for the Gills, though, that the devastation they were feeling would not last long, and that they'd find strength in Dan's memory rather than despair or hopelessness in his absence. Of course, Hugh's thoughts turned to Dan and Anibel, too, and the happiness they'd discovered in each other. As for Anibel herself, he felt this was more than any essentially good person should have to bear—first with his own sudden abandonment of her, then with her failed marriage, and now with this unthinkable event. He'd seen a lifetime's worth of tragedy and bad luck in the Pacific, but this somehow seemed worse, and it was certainly more personal.

He now saw Anibel walking down Prospect Street. She wore a tan raincoat and a maroon headscarf. Before she crossed onto the Green, she stopped and spoke briefly to a foot patrolman who, apparently in answer to a question from her, shook his head. As she crossed the street, she caught sight of Hugh and rushed to him. She cried for a long time into his chest, and when she stopped they sat on the bench together. Around them, the city was already well into its busy Tuesday morning. No one took much note of the priest and the woman together on the park bench, and Hugh, normally self-conscious, gave it no thought at all.

Anibel wiped her eyes and nose.

"I don't understand what happened," she said.

Hugh told her all he knew. He said that the person who did it must have thought, very wrongly, that if he took Dan out of the picture, the damning articles in the newspaper would stop running.

"It has to be the one Dan mentioned to me," she said. "He said he was about the only one left out on the loose."

"Creasy."

"Yes. Dan said he was truly unbalanced. He said he had a mixture of being volatile and stupid. Everyone was afraid of what he might do, even his own men. I think Dan was afraid, too. I said to him that he should come stay with me—no, first I told him he should quit his job, then I told him to come stay because they didn't know about me. But he said no because my landlady would object. *My landlady*!

Anibel broke down again. Hugh took her hands and cried for a while, too. An elderly couple from Hugh's old neighborhood came out of the church and passed their bench.

"Our condolences, Father," the man said.

Word was out. Hugh thanked them and dried his own eyes. Anibel was now looking at him plainly.

"What am I supposed to do now?" she asked.

Hugh had no ready answer.

"One foot in front of the other," he said without much conviction. "Let's hope the police do their job. Everyone who loved Danny will have a chance to remember him and pay their respects."

Hugh didn't think now was the time to bring up what he and Dan had discovered about Sandy Jones and his possible tie-in to Murphy the chauffeur and possibly the Wheelers. It would be too confusing for her, too out of the blue. He glanced back at her and saw that she was still looking at him.

"No, Hugh," she said. "I mean what am I—me, Anibel Moss—what am *I* supposed to do now? Dan was going to be my best friend for the rest of my life."

It went like that for another half-hour. Hugh offered the sanctuary of the church and of his own imperfect friendship at any time. He said he was going up to the Gills and that she was welcome to come, but she said she'd not spoken to them since she and Danny had gotten together, and to show up now would feel a little uncomfortable. She said she'd go to her office for a while, and call her parents, and that she'd be available either there or at home if Hugh heard anything. They embraced once more and then went their separate ways.

Hugh let himself in the Gills' front door without knocking. There were several cars parked out on the street, family mostly, and the sounds of multiple conversations as he came through into the entrance hall. The scent of cinnamon drifted from the kitchen at the end of the long hallway. Coffee cakes in the oven. One of Dan's sisters, Anne, walked out of a side room, saw Hugh, and came to give him a long hug.

"Dad," she called over his shoulder, "Hugh's here."

With that, others emerged to greet him, too. There was

a strong sense that busyness—baking, cooking, answering the phone, fussing over the dog, going out for ice—was already shaping the horrible, jagged pain of Dan's death into something more manageable. The logistics of the funeral home, the church, a singer, the cemetery, the caterer, the obituary for the newspaper, the phoning of distant friends—it all worked to apply numbing ice to the bruising reality, although every few minutes one of them would remember something that Dan had once said, or see his photo on a shelf, and have to go find a seat in a quiet corner of the house.

Dr. Gill came down the stairs. He looked like he hadn't slept at all.

"So good of you to come, Hugh," he said, extending his arms. "The police got the guy."

"Creasy?"

"Yes. He was on his way out of town. They got him at the Shell station on West Main Street. His bag was packed and in the car. He had a gun on the seat beside him."

"No resistance?"

"No, they apparently really surprised him."

"I don't think he'll ever see the light of day again."

"I hope not," said Dr. Gill.

Hugh thought the police might now get to the bottom of everything else, too, unless Creasy was one of those stubborn silent types. Punks with big ideas are sometimes like that, he thought, but the police might be persuasive.

"Is Dan's mother upstairs?" Hugh asked.

"Yes, she's in our room, just resting in an armchair. She's tired but she'd love to see you."

The master bedroom was large, with windows that looked out on the hillside all the way down to the center of town. Mrs. Gill was gazing out one of the windows. She turned and brightened just a little when she saw it was Hugh knocking gently on the open door.

"Father, please come in and sit," she said. She'd always been more formal than the rest of her family when it came to Hugh.

He took both her hands into his own and leaned down to her.

"It's such a terrible, shocking loss for all of us," he said.

"Yes, it is," she said. "Thank you. We're all in need of your blessings. I've never said this out loud, but he was my favorite."

She paused before continuing on. "Now I'd like to go over some arrangements with you," she said.

No one could push a tragedy deeper into a closet than Mrs. Gill. Dan once explained that it was the Irish in her. She would mourn in due time, but right now there were other considerations to take care of in order to make things right for her son. She asked Hugh to celebrate the funeral mass Thursday, if he felt able, and give a blessing at the wake Wednesday evening and a prayer at the burial when the time came. Dan said he wouldn't have it any other way.

"Good, now I don't have to worry about any of that," Mrs. Gill said. "It's best to get it all done swiftly, I think. We have to be strong for Dan."

"Yes."

"He'll mock us if we aren't."

Hugh smiled at that. Mrs. Gill stood to go join the others downstairs.

"What about Miss Moss?" she asked. "Have you told her?"

"Yes, I told her early this morning."

"How did she take it?"

"Not well. They'd really fallen in love, even after all these years. They were ready to let the world know. I think they would have gotten married."

Mrs. Gill put a steadying hand on the back of the chair.

"Where is she now?"

"She said she was going to work. I don't know where else she has to go. Maybe her parents will come down from Maine to be with her."

"She can't be by herself in her office, Hugh. Call her and tell her to come join us. The activity will do her good. She needs other people right now and we need her."

As always, she was right. If Hugh didn't have his hospital rounds to make, he probably would have stayed, too. There was no levity in the house, of course—not with a death so unexpected and horrifying—but there was warmth and intimacy and a shared understanding of who Dan was and how his loss would be so difficult to bear. Hugh reached Anibel at her office. He told her first about the capture of Creasy, then the arrangements for Dan's wake and funeral, and finally that she should come up to the Gills, where everyone was hoping to see her.

"Do they know about Dan and me?" Anibel asked.

"Yes. You apparently didn't do as good a job of hiding it as you thought."

"Do you know if they approved?"

"Just come up, Anibel. You'll feel better and certainly less alone the minute you walk through the door. I'll wait until you get here."

So Anibel took a taxi up the hill and joined in the family circle at the Gill house. As the day wore on, she and others, especially Dan's two sisters, drank wine and shared stories. Somehow, in the universal manner of younger sisters, Meg and Anne knew all the details of their brother's relationship with Anibel going all the way back to high school. Anibel was grateful for their shared sadness, something she realized she wouldn't have been able to bear on her own. She stayed until quite late, until one of Dan's brothers, still a student in college, gave her a ride home.

CHAPTER 11

The last thing Waterbury needed that week in August was another big storm, but that's what it was going to get. The certainty came on Wednesday, when forecasters began referring to the approaching Hurricane Diane in apocalyptic terms. The ground, they noted, was already saturated from recent rains, and standing water remained at street intersections, on ballfields and in basements. Trees were certain to topple in the coming high winds, and highways would be impassable. Hurricane Connie would seem like nothing once Diane came through.

Although Hugh remained in a state of shaken disbelief regarding Dan, he could feel the city's nervous mood as he walked to get the mail on Wednesday. The sun hadn't been out in days—an unusual occurrence for August—and the endless clouds seemed to have put a lid over the valley. The smoke from its many billowing stacks had nowhere to go. The pounding of machinery through open factory windows and the coupling of rail cars in the yards were muffled by the heavy, sultry air, and their strange echoes seemed to carry notes of foreboding as they disappeared into the surrounding hills. But it was the grayness of everything that got deepest into Hugh's unhappy mood. Gone was the usual palette of summer colors. The skies, the buildings and the people were all now uniformly gray, the dull color of the pigeons that rose and fell with depressing regularity out on the Waterbury Green.

Even as he made plans for what he would say at Dan's wake, funeral and burial, Hugh was plagued by the idea that he might have been responsible for his friend's death. He thought of it now as he walked once again past Jimmy's Heel Bar and the memory of Teddy Valuckas and everything that followed. What if Valuckas hadn't slipped out of the confessional that Saturday? What if he'd come by the rectory and confessed a few days later? Would Danny still be alive? It was hard to make all the connections. If Valuckas had gone under confession's seal, Hugh could only have been a by-stander instead of a participant in all that came next. Of course, Dan was already working on the story at the time. He easily might have come to Valuckas on his own. Or maybe he never would have known about him at all and instead would have successfully re-ported the story from another angle. It was impossible to know, but Hugh profoundly regretted opening his mouth that June night on the Gills' back porch—not only for Dan's sake, but for Dan and Anibel and the future they might have had together.

Hugh was also quite sure that his reckoning with the Church hierarchy would be coming soon. Everyone in the rec-tory, including Msgr. Shutt, had been solicitous and kind in the hours following Dan's murder, with their prayers, condolences and offers of help flowing freely. But the fact remained that he had got himself caught up in a police investigation and had per-haps cavalierly mishandled a man's admission of guilt and wish to confess. Some sort of punishment or reprimand would surely be coming down from above. Hugh wondered about his reputation and his standing among the other priests. Could he really stay on at the Immaculate under such circumstances? And, anyway, was this comfortable, well connected life in Waterbury the thing that had initially called out to him so forcefully back in the Phil-ippines? He felt as if he were going terribly astray. Not that he wanted to leave the priesthood—he remained dedicated to that—but maybe it was time to go out into the world again. With Dan gone and Anibel a complicated presence, maybe he should move along. After all, how many more times could he walk past the shoeshine parlor on Leavenworth Street before he lost his mind?

Lots to consider, everything to consider, thought Hugh, but first things first.

◆ ◆ ◆

The wake, a traditional Irish affair, was held under the watchful eyes of the Kerry brothers in their rooms on Willow Street. Owing to the nature of Dan's wounds, the casket was closed. Because he was unmarried, his parents were the ones who stood at the head of the receiving line, followed in age order by his siblings. Under the protocol, Anibel could stand nearby but not in the line itself. Not that she wanted to. Most people, unaware of her changed status with Dan, would have wondered what in the world she was doing there and then jumped to all sorts of conclusions. Meanwhile, the line of those wishing to pay respects stretched for hours out the door and up the street. These were longtime and short-term friends of Dan and his family, acquaintances, neighbors, co-workers of Dan at the newspaper and his father at the hospital, many of the curious who'd been drawn by the grisly details of the murder, and a well-known few who turned up at wakes and funerals all across the city as a perverse form of recreation. The mayor made a quick but dignified appearance, trailed by the usual retinue of lesser elected and appointed officials. The Police and Fire departments sent along uniformed, white-gloved contingents, with the promise of the same again at Thursday's funeral. Everyone considered that to be a marvelous and memorable gesture.

Hugh's plan was to make himself present and available for the entire wake, which ran from 4 to 9 p.m. with an hour's break for a bite to eat at 6. Many of those coming through knew of his lifelong friendship with Dan and greeted him with a "Very sorry for your loss," and perhaps a bit more. Hugh noted how hushed and sad the line was as it snaked through the parlors, with none of the bright talk and laughter that could mark the passing of longer, well-lived life. Before he was to offer his prayer, he snuck back to the smoking room for a quick puff. A couple of men there were raising shot glasses of Jameson, poured from a bottle someone had thoughtfully left on a side table. One of the men was Detective Walker, who'd come to Kerry's separately from the official police contingent to offer his respects to the Gills. The other man left the room, but Walker stayed behind to talk to Hugh.

"We had a bead on him, Father," the detective said, shaking his head. "We thought we could get him before he could do any more damage."

His tone was apologetic, which Hugh thought unusual for a cop.

"How do you get everyone but the ringleader?" Hugh asked. He was convinced the police had done, and were still doing, an inadequate job.

"That's the way it usually goes. You start at the bottom and work your way up. We had enough on him to bring him in. We just couldn't find him."

"It's not such a big city, for someone to be able to lose himself like that."

"You'd be surprised."

Hugh wondered if he should bring up the Jones-Murphy connection. He'd spoken over the phone with Sandy Jones earlier in the day, and they'd agreed to meet at his house on Friday, once all the arrangements having to do with Dan were over with. Jones had asked again about baptism, but Hugh had urged patience, saying he needed to hear more from Jones about his character and commitment before taking the next steps.

"Will Creasy talk?" Hugh asked Walker. "He's a murderer. There's no doubt he killed Dan. But I can't believe he's an art thief. Someone put him up to it."

"He's all zipped up," said Walker. "But it's possible he was getting his orders from the chauffeur, too, and that he never knew who was at the top."

Hugh decided not to tell Walker about Jones. He'd go talk to him alone. He wouldn't involve anyone else. It was obvious from Jones' recent visit to the rectory that he had a story to tell. Maybe, if Hugh gave him a chance, he'd say too much. And until he'd officially been baptized—if that ever was going to happen—

he wasn't entitled to protection under the rules of confession. It was a variation on the roundabout he'd had with Valuckas, Hugh thought, but it might work in his favor this time. He stubbed out his cigarette and wished Walker well. He promised to pass along any information he heard. Then he returned to Kerry's big room and spoke his brief prayer for poor Danny's soul.

◆ ◆ ◆

It was already raining on Thursday morning as Hugh took a seat at the rectory's meeting table along with all the other priests and staff. Msgr. Shutt had called the meeting in light of the dire weather forecast. He wanted to offer the church basement as a public shelter in case of flooding or a widespread loss of power. Unbeknownst to most parishioners, the Immaculate already had a large supply of water, food, blankets and cots stored away. Earlier in the decade, Shutt's predecessor had become determined that the church and congregation should be able to survive what he saw as an inevitable nuclear attack. Now, facing another sort of calamity, the church could make the supplies he'd purchased—and power from its own generator—available to the community. Father Fox had quietly been put in charge of organizing and implementing the plan. There were volunteers from the parish who could be called upon on short notice. In fact, cots were being set up and water kegs moved into place even as they spoke. All priests and parish personnel, including the nuns at St. Mary's School, were expected to take part and help out if it came to that. As of right now, it looked like the worst weather would be coming Friday night. Until then, Masses would continue to be said and Communion offered in the church as per the existing schedule.

All of this barely registered on Hugh. The initial shock of Dan's death had by now lessened somewhat, but he wasn't quite ready for a Civil Defense lesson, however worthy. At the moment, his sights were set on that afternoon's funeral mass for Dan. He had trouble keeping focused. He knew that in order to prepare properly for the ceremony, he had to get away from the church and rectory, away from everything, to be alone with his thoughts for a while. In days past, getting away for personal reflection often meant a climb up to the top of Waterbury's Pine Hill, a treeless, rock-strewn, uninhabitable prominence on the city's south end. Hugh thought it was the loneliest, most monkish place in Waterbury. It always reminded him of Ireland's Hill of Ben, a windswept peak set between two lakes just northwest of Dublin, and the site of legendary sermons during the early days of Christianity. But now Pine Hill was undergoing a transformation. A local man had somehow gotten hold of the property and was almost single-handedly creating a miniature version of the Holy Land there. Using everyday materials such as concrete and chicken wire and various discarded household items, he was building crude depictions of places and scenes from the Old and New Testaments. According to his feverish vision, the display would attract pilgrims from all around the Northeast and promote a better understanding of the Christian faith. His determination was admirable, but he had a long way to go, Hugh thought. In the meantime, the solitude and serenity of the hillside was now a thing of the past.

Instead, Hugh headed to a vest-pocket park located very near his old neighborhood and only a few steps north of downtown. Hayden Park was little used, largely because it could be accessed only by a daunting flight of stone steps from the street below or an entrance walk hidden between two houses from above. Even so, as boys, Hugh and Dan had spent many afternoons in the park's ample shade, where they could smoke a stick of punk with no one to see, or mischievously tinker with the fountain that fed the park's central wading pool, jamming in a Popsicle stick and sending a geyser of water high into the air. Even now, from beneath an umbrella on a rainy day in August, it seemed like an appropriate place for Hugh to sit and consider what lessons, if any, he could draw from Dan's death for his sermon.

The tendency of the Church was to try to soften the blow of death beneath a thick blanket of incense, holy water, solemn liturgical music and the soothing ebb and flow of unintelligible

Latin words. But that wouldn't do for Dan, Hugh thought. It wouldn't be enough. Or maybe it would be too much. Dan was 30, just coming into his own, but now cruelly taken down, like a young cowboy in a song. After all they'd seen and experienced in the war, and how grateful they'd been to get out alive, it seemed terribly unfair. Dan's weapon against Creasy had been a typewriter and an admirable sense of right and wrong, but Creasy's weapon was a gun. Again, unfair. Dan's side might eventually get the last word, but he wouldn't be around to enjoy it. Hugh looked out at the rain. What was wrong with the world? What good had all the prayers done? Waterbury no longer seemed like the place where they'd grown up together, or even the place where they'd celebrated Easter just a few months earlier. Hugh realized that his thoughts were drifting. He was very tired. He couldn't address any of these complicated, difficult feelings during the funeral mass—not directly, anyway. He listened to the rainwater splash into the wading pool. Water upon water. He was the only one in the park. He settled himself. He knew his job at the service was to comfort rather than provoke. He could do that, *would* do it. He was good at it. But his promise to himself was that he'd somehow get to the same evil core that Dan had been driving toward and expose it for all to see.

The Gills and others, mostly close friends, who were interested were to meet at 2 p.m. at the funeral home, from which they'd depart for the 3 p.m. funeral mass. The afternoon service was unusual, but it was the only time available once Mrs. Gill insisted that everything take place as promptly as possible. Hugh got there a little early, again to console others, give a brief benediction and ride with Dan's casket to the church. He'd called Anibel to see if she wanted to come with him to Kerry's, but she'd said no.

"I spent enough time there yesterday," she'd said. "You can

only do it for so long. Besides, there'll be enough mumbo-jumbo at the church without my having to listen to you pray over Dan at the funeral parlor."

Her voice sounded distant and strained. For once, though, he was happy to hear her disparage his calling. It meant she'd recovered a little. She said the Gills had asked her to be with them but that she'd go to the funeral with the Barbers and the Dahls, old Crosby friends who knew Dan well and loved him.

"How are you doing today?" Hugh asked.

"My obsessive thought right now is that I never got to see Dan or say goodbye to him," she said. "I found myself talking to the casket last night. I don't even know if he's really in there. I began imagining where else he could be. I thought maybe back in Italy. How are you doing?"

"About the same," Hugh said. "At least I have duties to perform. I'm not sure what comes after that."

"He was doing what he loved," she said after a pause.

"Yes, he was."

As the Gills, all in variations of black, came into the funeral home, Hugh saw a good family struggling to be at its best. Dan's mother and dad smiled gamely as they encountered familiar faces, most of whom they'd seen the day before. Dan's brother, Tim, had just made it in several hours earlier from West Berlin, where, judging by his vague descriptions, Hugh thought he must be working for the CIA. Tim was now getting big hellos from the old crowd. Hugh again thanked Dan's sisters for comforting Anibel on the worst day of her life. They said it was Anibel who'd ended up comforting them.

At last it was time for the short ride to the Immaculate. Hugh rode shotgun in the hearse, with Dan's immediate family in the first car behind. In back of that came the long line of people driving their own cars, their headlights shining blearily in the rain to indicate they were part of a funeral procession and thus not subject to normal traffic laws. After arriving at the church's front entrance, Hugh accompanied the casket up the long set of steps and into the dry entranceway. He then walked quickly up a side aisle toward the sacristy, where he'd change into his vestments.

The rain hadn't kept many away. The big church was crowded and would probably be full in another 15 minutes. Hugh was to be assisted on the altar by two other priests; one was the Immaculate's own Aloysius Logue, another favorite of Dan's mother, while the other was an old family friend of the Gills, a Jesuit who'd taught Dan a memorable Dickens class at Fordham. Hugh glanced at the program to reinforce in his mind the order of things, although most was well proscribed by tradition. The photo of Dan on the front of the program showed him sitting at a portable desk in what looked like the middle of the North African desert. On the desk were his typewriter, a ream of copy paper, a Thermos and a tin cup. He was shirtless, dog-tagged, tanned and smiling broadly, looking back over his shoulder at the camera. He'd probably never been so happy in his life. Hugh folded the program and put it in a pocket. He went over the order of things with the two altar boys and then, at the opening strains of "Be Not Afraid," walked out to the altar.

The ceremony did what it needed to do. The music was familiar and well performed, the two readings were brief and stirring. Hugh, the altar boys and the two other priests moved with what appeared to all to be a graceful and well-rehearsed choreography. According to Catholic custom, the presiding priest would give the only eulogy. At the Immaculate, the ornate, gilded pulpit was rather ostentatiously located atop a spiral staircase that wound around one of the big marble pillars at the front of the church. Hugh disliked the high and mighty feeling the pulpit gave him as he loomed over the congregation, and he felt his echoing words were often lost in the vast upper reaches of the nave rather than making it all the way down to the pews. He would go extra slowly and succinctly today.

"I should start out by advising you never to use the word 'deceased' when referring to Daniel Gill," he began. "I don't know how many times he told me what an inadequate word he thought it was. 'You're not *deceased*, Hugh,' he'd say. 'You're *dead*, and there's no use sugarcoating it.' So spoke a true newspaperman, a lover of plain language and plain facts, and my dear lifelong friend. And so, we, the aggrieved, must say it today: Daniel Gill is dead."

Hugh's very personal, quite informal eulogy was well received, even though he intended it mostly for the ears of one who could no longer hear, and maybe for one other who could. The Gills were especially grateful for Hugh's tone and the generous breadth of his recollections, a good number of which included them. With the burial not scheduled right away, many in the crowd moved directly from the church to the reception at the nearby Waterbury Club. Hugh was among the last to arrive. He moved politely but purposefully through the crowd until he spotted Anibel in a cluster of friends by the club's big second-floor enclosed porch. She'd been looking out for him, too.

"That was really good," she told him, separating herself from her group and putting a hand on his forearm. "Just the right balance. I think it helped a lot. I know it helped me."

Hugh was relieved to get Anibel's approval. He thanked her.

"I just wanted to say something that he could have listened to without getting sick or walking out," Hugh said.

"I think you probably succeeded," Anibel said and took a sip of punch.

"I'm going to see Sandy Jones tomorrow," Hugh said after a moment. "I think he could well be tied into this whole mess. Dan thought so, too."

"Dan mentioned something to me on the phone the other night—the last thing he said to me, almost—but I can't take any of it in right now," Anibel said. "I've decided I'm going to get away for a little bit. It means I'll miss the burial, which I really don't need to see, but my parents are right on the ocean in Maine and I think that's where I would like to be right now."

"Of course," said Hugh. "Understood. I've booked a spot in September at our retreat house on the shore. Let the salt air work its magic."

Anibel gave Hugh her parents' number so he could call with

any news. He said he wouldn't call unless it was something big. Then they parted, knowing they'd see each other again soon. Hugh stayed for another hour, said his goodbyes, remembered his umbrella and walked back home quickly, almost running, through the rain.

◆ ◆ ◆

It was dinnertime when he got to the rectory, but he was far too agitated to eat. He didn't go to his room, but rather to a small, infrequently used reading room on the third floor. He closed the door behind him as he entered, sat down in a swiveling armchair, put his head back and closed his eyes.

The key to unlocking the great puzzle had come to him all at once, right in the middle of Dan's funeral Mass. Indeed, it had come to him at the very holiest part of the Mass, as he strained a bit to lift the gold chalice above his head and intoned the Latin words that recognized the miraculous transubstantiation —the turning of wine into Christ's blood. If he'd been facing the congregation, an astute observer might have seen the widening of Hugh's eyes as the pieces clicked into place, but he was high on the altar, facing away. No one heard his tiny, involuntary yelp of recognition, either. Closest were the altar boys kneeling several levels below him, one with his head devoutly bowed and the other concerned only with ringing his bell at exactly the transforming moment.

Now, at last alone in a room, Hugh could think the whole thing through. It made such perfect sense that he was amazed that he or anyone else hadn't thought of it earlier. It didn't supply answers to all the questions, but it would go a very long way. His only problem now would be keeping everything to himself until his meeting the next day with Sandy Jones.

CHAPTER 12

By Friday morning, Hurricane Diane was unloading its full force on Western Connecticut. The storm was reportedly creeping slowly somewhere just off to the south, picking up moisture from the ocean and dumping it onto already swollen inland waterways. The rain in Waterbury was now steady and heavy, and it was expected to stay that way for another 24 hours. Moderate flooding was already being reported in low lying areas, and a persistent wind was swaying treetops and loudly whipping flags on their various standards around downtown. The early Masses at the Immaculate had almost a nautical aspect: Attendees straggled in, soaked through to the skin, as if from the stormy deck of a ship, while the wind sighed and the rain pounded the stained-glass windows way up high. Hugh's service was interrupted repeatedly by the sound of a door or shutter banging against its frame somewhere deep down in the bowels of the church.

Hugh was grateful that he had a Mass to say. Even during the brisk early morning services, he found a restful place in the rituals and familiar cadences, and in the faces of the devout as they took the wafer. For a moment or two, he even might have forgotten what the afternoon held in store: his 2 p.m. meeting with Jones, the springing of his theory, and who knew what after that.

After Mass, he looked for ways to further occupy himself and thus speed the clock. He ate Mrs. Dunn's eggs and toast deliberately and read every page of two newspapers. Then he went back to the church and down into the basement to look in on the preparations being made for the storm. No refugees had yet taken up residence, but by 11 a.m. volunteers were already at their stations, drinking coffee and listening anxiously to the radio. The waiting reminded Hugh of when he was a boy and the father of one of his Driggs friends was running for mayor of Waterbury, and he'd gone with his friend to the campaign headquarters to await the results on election night. They drank orange soda and ate ham-and-mustard sandwiches on hard rolls as the tallies came in by phone. A radio was reporting the vote as well. The hanging around was excruciating because nothing more could be done to affect the outcome. Everything was up to the voters, and they'd already voted and gone home. Similarly, in the Immaculate's basement, the act of waiting itself had turned into its own tense drama. The fate of hundreds, maybe thousands, was riding on an ever-churning and -changing low-pressure system that no one could do anything about. Hugh wondered if voters were more or less fickle than the weather. As he moved from battle station to battle station, he told the workers vaguely that he'd be back later. He'd signed up for the overnight shift. As he walked out, he recognized that he wasn't really engaging with people as he normally did. He was just floating along, still trying to adjust to Dan's brutal absence.

As he drove around the Green and out East Main Street for his rounds at St. Mary's, he saw that a number of stores hadn't bothered to open their doors. The grocery was open, along with the newsstands, smoke shops and a diner or two, but the clothing stores and other larger retailers—places where purchases could wait a day or two—were shuttered. The hospital was, of course, in crisis mode, deep into the dictates of its natural-disaster protocols. Gurneys were lined up by the Emergency Room entrance. Medicines had been freshly stocked and plasma bags were ready to go. Hospital personnel had their own cots and food supplies set up in the basement as well. Everything seemed to be on a wartime footing. The decks were cleared. Smoke 'em if you got 'em. There was an extra charge in the nurses' banter.

Hugh had only a few patients to see, none in critical condition. In the maternity ward, he stuck his head in to say hello to Mrs. Phelan, who was propped up on pillows and sucking ice chips, well into a difficult labor for what would be child number twelve.

"If it's a girl, you'll have to name her Diane, won't you?" he said cheerily.

"Diane?"

"After the storm."

She looked at him with a weary smile that wished him away. Hugh offered a hasty blessing for mother and child and then made his way back out to his car. He'd managed to fill a potentially tension-ridden morning and mid-day with a stubbornly by-the-book priestly routine, but now he was splashing back along East Main Street to Sandy Jones' house. He finally allowed his thoughts to switch over fully to the task ahead. He was reminded of the morning he'd been lined up with his fellow paratroopers, ready to jump out of an airplane and into the Los Banos prison camp. Back then, he'd asked the blessing of God. Now he felt the favor of a couple of mortals as well. First, there was Anibel, whom he hoped was running ahead of the storm on her way up to Maine. And then there was the acute presence of Danny, whose very active spirit seemed to be doing everything but actually steering the car up Prospect Street and into Sandy Jones' driveway.

Jones greeted Hugh at the kitchen door and ushered him through to the interior of the house.

"Please forgive the genteel poverty," he said with a wave of his hand as he went. Again, as he'd started out during his rectory visit, he spoke with a studied boarding-school nonchalance.

The house had a stripped-down, burglarized feel, as if pieces of furniture, rugs and wall hangings, once prominent, had somehow gone missing. The rooms were dim, high-ceilinged, dusty and forlorn. They were certainly bachelor quarters, but in a house that was way too big for them—and everything was coated and darkened by decades of cigarette smoke and neglect. They at last came to a corner of the enormous sunken living room where armchairs sat on each side of an ornate old three-bulb floor lamp lit up at top wattage against the lowering darkness outside. Jones gestured toward one of the chairs.

"Can I get you anything?" he asked.

"No, thanks," said Hugh, taking a seat.

"Good. I'm running out of things to offer. No more good sherry, or even glasses to put it in."

He was about to say more, but Hugh held up a hand to stop him.

"Before you say whatever it is you want to say, I'm going to begin with something of my own," he said.

Jones sat down opposite him and casually crossed his legs. Hugh resumed.

"No one ever intended to keep those paintings that were taken from the Wheelers that night, did they?" he said.

"I don't understand."

"I think you do. The target that night wasn't the paintings. It was the frames they were in."

Jones thrust out his chin bravely.

"I don't know what you mean," he said.

"It hit me yesterday, while I was saying the funeral Mass for Dan Gill. I was lifting the chalice toward the tabernacle, thinking for the hundredth time how surprisingly heavy solid gold is, when everything fell into place. Why so many strong hands were needed at the Wheelers to remove the paintings from the walls and out the door. Why one painting was left behind. Why the canvases were returned undamaged. Why local thieves would ever get involved in the first place. It was gold, Sandy. The answer is gold. And who of all people might have known the frames were solid gold in the first place? You, Sandy. Maybe a few others. I doubt it, though. Even Seth and Alice Wheeler apparently didn't realize it. But your family—fathers, grandfathers—goes way back with the Wheelers, in and out of each other's houses for decades. Plus, you're the one with the motive. You're the one being blackmailed and in desperate need of cash. It was you, Sandy. Only you."

Jones suddenly had nowhere to go. His initial plan had been to continue to seek an expedited baptism from Hugh, and then a secure confession and blanket forgiveness. He didn't really know how it all worked, how the Church decided such things, and he didn't have a back-up strategy. Maybe simply beginning a conversation would lead to something.

"You know me," he began.

"I don't really know you, no," said Hugh.

"Well, you know about me."

"I'm learning about you."

Hugh saw that Jones was now going off script.

"I'm not sure about all I said to you when I came to your building the other night," Jones said, "but I know I unburdened myself to some degree."

"Yes."

"Did I mention that I was being blackmailed?"

"Not in so many words, but I assumed it by what you said."

Jones paused, as if considering his next move.

"Are you sure you don't want anything, Hugh? I can make a cup of tea."

"No, I'm fine."

"Yes, the frames were gold," Jones said.

"You say 'were.'"

"Oh, I'm sure they've been cashed in and melted down by now."

Hugh let Jones continue.

"Old man Wheeler—C.C., Seth's grandfather—knew how to make money, even as a young man, but he faced some setbacks as well. When he was 20, he lost his job during a financial collapse. Fifteen years later, he was hurt by the Panic of 1873. He never forgot how that felt. When his son began sending back paintings from France, he selected a handful of his favorites to hang in his new house here in Waterbury. Later on, in a moment of indiscretion, he confided in my own grandfather Jones—a close friend and a very rich man himself—that he'd had four large frames made of solid gold as a hedge against another financial calamity. For decades, they just hung there in plain sight. In his old age, with perhaps a touch of senility, my grandfather, who I was close to, told me about old man Wheeler and the frames. I'm sure he thought I'd never have to worry about money. He certainly thought I could be trusted. But, alas, he was wrong on both counts, and there you have it."

"No one ever told Seth Wheeler?"

"Apparently not. His father probably knew, but he died young, without warning, and I guess he never arrived at the right moment to pass the secret along. They might have found out themselves, but they never moved those paintings and so never realized how heavy they were. Seth saw them as sort of a shrine to his father and grandfather and kept them in place. Just dusted them occasionally. Rather silly, really."

"And you never told them."

"Why would I? They've never approved of me, and that's going all the way back. Something about me always rubbed them, all of them, the wrong way, even in grade school. They thought I didn't fit in, and I didn't, but they punished me for it. Seth Wheeler wouldn't tell me if I was about to be run over by a train."

Jones was speaking quietly and matter-of-factly, clearly relishing the details of what he, and only he, knew.

"You know, Sandy, you're speaking to me without any sort of confidentiality right now," Hugh said. "This isn't by any means a protected confession in the eyes of the Church."

"I understand that. I do know that much. It's just that I have so much to regret and be ashamed of—so much awful behavior—and no one to tell. You're cheaper than a shrink. I'll leave it to you to sort out."

Again, Hugh said nothing, and Jones resumed.

"There are certain things you can do and certain other things you can't do. You can be a drunk and a cheat and a fornicator, and that's all fine—you can probably get away with it in one way or another. But those things were always too commonplace for me, Hugh, so in recent years I've crossed over into one of the real taboos. Youngsters. Children, really. That seemed to be a depraved enough thing for me to do. Even hardened criminals hate you for doing that. They'll kill you in prison for that. I just closed my eyes and took the plunge."

Hugh wanted to leap out of his chair at him.

"But then others found out," he said.

"Yes."

"Creasy."

"Yes, him. An awful, bloodthirsty person. Worse than me. I was far from discreet, I will admit, and yet this was something I really couldn't allow to get out generally, as you can imagine. One of the local purveyors of what I was looking for told someone who told someone else, and the next thing you knew I was being held up for regular payments, and then again and again. I still possessed just enough of a shred of my own respectability that I kept paying up."

With the rain continuing to come down in sheets outside, and rumbles of thunder coming through, Jones then told the story of the theft. He had no more money of his own and no more possessions of value. ("I stopped paying my dues and bills at the country club three years ago and no one has ever called me to account," he said.) He was basically down to zero. Creasy didn't accept that. He started roughing him up and threatening him, so finally in desperation Jones told him about the frames. Together, they did the planning with the help of Thomas Murphy, whose own gambling debts Jones had covered years earlier, and who'd consequently become beholden to him. Creasy supplied the muscle, Jones the knowledge and Murphy the access. Murphy was supposed to have been paid off and allowed to leave town for Cuba, but, unbeknownst to Jones, a distrusting Creasy had him killed on the spot by Valuckas.

"At that point, I'd become involved in murder—I considered Murphy a friend—and things were beginning to spin out of control," Jones said. "The big story appeared in the newspaper and then I saw Ted Valuckas talking to you one morning downtown."

"You saw that?"

"I was getting my shoes shined. You saw me but you didn't see me. By the way he was gesturing, and you were reacting, I could tell he was saying too much. Reporting him was the worst thing I did, but he had to go. I thought things would get back to normal after that. I don't know who killed him or how."

"And Dan Gill?"

"Trust me, I had nothing to do with that."

Hugh decided not to trace for Jones the line that led directly from his perversions to Danny's death.

"Is that everything?" he asked.

"I guess so."

"The Whistler that wasn't taken?"

"It doesn't have a gold frame, only gilded. It was purchased and hung after the old man died."

"Three men have been murdered," Hugh said. "Most or all of the guilty parties are in custody. Creasy will probably tell everything at some point, probably very soon, to try and keep himself out of the electric chair. When will you go to the police? Everyone needs to hear your story, not just me."

"You'll be happy to know that Detective Walker and I have an appointment for 10 o'clock tomorrow morning. I wish I could just tell them half the story—the crime without the shame. I can't believe how the whole thing snowballed. They were going to take the frames and return the canvases to me. Period. Which they did. The gold was worth over $100,000 to them. Creasy was supposed to leave me alone. But then murder followed murder, and Creasy came back to me, demanding even more. I could see it was never going to end. It isn't the sort of situation I was built for, Hugh."

"What do you expect me to do now?" Hugh asked. He was very ready to leave.

"You're a priest. You do what you do. Baptize me."

Hugh stood.

"You know, Sandy, when you appeared at the rectory, I asked you what you were afraid of, and you told me about the blackmailers and the beatings," he said. "But seeing you now, I realize that's not it. It's hell that you're most afraid of, isn't it?"

"I've been thinking about it, yes. I'm not well, you know."

"And the whole country club thing—that's what it was really all about. You needed a friend in a collar, someone who could forgive your behavior."

"It was more than just that."

"But it was that, too."

"Yes."

"The Church doesn't close its door to anyone, or almost anyone," Hugh said. "But nothing happens until you see the police in the morning."

Hugh let himself out Jones' back door and drove down the hill. Once back at the rectory, he went to his room, hoping to find a quiet hour or two. He tried to prepare his Sunday sermon, and then switched over to reading, but it was impossible to concentrate on those things. He was devastated not to have Dan to call. He knew the whole story now, but didn't have anyone to tell about it, at least not yet. He could only listen to the storm rage and build. He'd told Anibel that he'd call her with big news —which this certainly was—but he couldn't bring himself to do it. She was a strong and resourceful woman, but she wasn't nearly herself when she'd left for her parents' house. If Jones was arrested tomorrow, as he surely had to be, he'd call her then. Would the news lift her feelings? Probably not, but it was a step in the right direction. At least a lot of the wondering would be over.

In the meantime, Hugh began to grow restless. His night shift in the church basement shelter was still hours away. The chalky face of Jones loomed before him—his rouged cheeks, painted hair and sunken frame reminded Hugh of a ventriloquist's grotesque dummy. They say that a man afraid of hell, and close enough to it to feel its warmth, will tell his whole story, and that's pretty much what Jones had done. He probably could have told more if Hugh had stuck around and been able to stomach it. But he didn't have to, so he didn't. Maybe Jones' confession to the police would lead to all sorts of other discoveries, but that was their job, not Hugh's. In fact, Hugh's job might again, finally, get back to where it belonged. He could return to being only a priest, albeit one who now would now feel more at a loss in the world than ever.

It was upon that thought that someone knocked on Hugh's door.

"There's a phone call for you downstairs, Father," the voice announced. "Miss Anibel Moss, calling long distance."

CHAPTER 13

"I don't know what I'm doing here with my parents," Anibel said straight away, sounding angrier with herself than with Hugh. "Why didn't you stop me from coming?"

"You're tired and you've been through hell," Hugh replied. "I thought you could stand to get away. I envied you, to tell you the truth."

"Well, as long as there's something I need to get away from, I probably shouldn't get away from it. I hope that makes sense. Anyway, I left you all alone and shouldn't have."

"Your spirit has been with me today."

"You can say that about a dead person, like Dan, but not about me. I'm still here. I'm coming back down in the morning. As soon as I got here, I was bored to death, so I called Alvin Walker. He was in a talkative mood. He told me that Sandy Jones was coming into headquarters. He said he wasn't sure why. I have to be there for that, Hugh."

"I spent an hour with Jones this afternoon," Hugh said, and then he went ahead and told the whole story of his visit. Anibel listened without interruption.

"My God, the gold frames—you made the hair stand up on the back of my neck," she said when he was finished. "It's so obvious when you know about it. You could have told me about that at the reception."

"I really wanted to, but I wasn't sure at that point. It was really just a guess on my part. I didn't think I should say anything until I went and talked to Jones."

"You could have told me as soon as you got back from seeing him. I gave you my parents' number for a reason."

"I was planning on calling you tomorrow, after he's arrested."

"Do you think he can be trusted to turn himself in?"

"You should see him. He's a wreck. He's not going anywhere. And, honestly, neither should you. What will you gain by coming back?"

"Please don't try to tell me what to do, Hugh. I just feel like I need to be there, probably for Dan. Wherever this all leads, I want to be there to represent him. Somehow, I got a second wind during the ride up here, and now I want to come back."

"Okay, Anibel. We're in the middle of a hurricane, you know."

"Well, I'd hate to miss that, too," she said. "I'm running up the phone bill here. I'll see you tomorrow."

Because of the storm and the needs of the shelter next door, dinner at the rectory was provided on an as-needed basis. Mrs. Dunn had stacked plates of cold chicken and potato salad in the Frigidaire for the priests to take out and eat as they were able. When Hugh got to the dining table, Father Logue was sitting alone, just finishing his meal. He was due back in the church basement but was never one to pass up an opportunity to tell a story, even to an audience of one. After exchanging a few pleasantries and concerns about the continuing poor weather, Logue found his opening.

"How well do you remember the Hurricane of '38?" he asked, refilling his glass with iced tea.

"Well enough," said Hugh. "I was 13, living just up the hill from here. I remember that we had a big chestnut tree in our back yard and all the chestnuts came down at once."

"This storm is reminding me of 1938," Logue went on.

"I was an associate pastor in Madison—St. Margaret's—and the wind and rain came on so suddenly and without warning that I got stuck in traffic out on the Boston Post Road. The traffic lights went out, branches started to fall onto the roads, and some people just stopped their cars right where they were and refused to go any further."

He paused for a moment, as if allowing the sounds of the storm outside to add color to his story.

"So there I was on the Post Road with nowhere to go. Not forward, not back, not sideways. The wind was ferocious. I remember that I had music, but mostly static, playing on the car radio. The station was going in and out. I was wondering how I might draw it all into a sermon, when there was a tremendous crack and a big oak tree fell down onto the car right in front of me. Missed me by 20 feet. Well, weather or no weather, I had to see what I could do. The car had been absolutely crushed. Some men and women from other cars came to help. There were downed wires, but we could get around them. We managed to get the driver-side door open at least partially. A woman was slumped over in the seat there. She'd taken a severe blow to the head. As far as we could see, she was lifeless. We pulled her out to see if she could be helped, and as we did so, a book fell from her lap and onto the pavement. She'd been reading while she was stuck in traffic."

He paused again for effect.

"The book was *Gone with the Wind*, Hugh. She'd been reading *Gone with the Wind*."

Hugh let the punchline sink in.

"That's quite a story, Father," he said. "Correct me if I'm wrong, but I have a feeling you've told it before."

"I think of it whenever there's a big storm like this," Father Logue said with an acknowledging nod. "There are always stories to be found in big storms. Everything's magnified. The unexpected happens—people's fortunes rising and falling, coincidences that seem pre-ordained, the devout seeing the hand of God in the good luck but never in the bad."

Hugh had often wondered about that, too. That kind of faith. A family is routed by a house fire and yet is thankful to God for only destroying everything they own while keeping them unharmed. "We were lucky," they invariably said.

"I agree," said Hugh. "They're like Bible stories that you live through—the scenes you'll never forget, the shared experiences, the close calls, the question of the Lord's role in it all."

"I may find a reason to retell my story on Sunday, Hugh. I hope not, but I'm beginning to think so."

By the time Father Logue made his way out of the rectory and over to the church basement, dusk had turned to night. Hugh went to the rectory library to await his turn in the shelter. He daydreamed a sermon about Noah's Flood and what lessons it could still hold for the modern world.

◆ ◆ ◆

It was as night fell on the region that the ground, all of it, completely gave up the job of absorbing any rainwater at all and began sending it straight into whatever brooks, streams or rivers were at hand. The accumulation of rain had already passed 12 inches in many spots, with still more on the way. The natural flow was, of course, from high to low and from north to south. The serious flooding had already started up by the Massachusetts border. Bridges were out and roads impassable in some of the small Litchfield County towns. Power lines along the dark country roads were down and unresponsive. Phone service was increasingly unreliable.

Every stream was full and racing to join others in the wild run south. Jake's Brook and Nickel Mine Brook, Troy Brook and High Meadow Brook, Pudding, Leadmine, Hancock and Steel—they were all rushing headlong as if with a single purpose: to join the Naugatuck River in the assault on the slumbering valley below.

At 11 p.m., Waterbury remained largely innocent of what

was headed its way. The local flooding remained spotty, although power outages from downed trees were becoming more common. People had been trickling into the shelter for a while. From his post by the coffee urns, Hugh noticed that they were mostly the familiar indigents who populated the downtown rooming houses and cheap hotels. Word of the free meals had gotten around. He suspected that many without power elsewhere in the city would ride it out at home. It was a fairly mild night in August, after all, not the same as one of those brutal February blizzards with people freezing to death in their own bedrooms.

Hugh enjoyed the easy rise and fall of conversations in the big hall as the hour got late. He thought this was the Church at its best, providing food, shelter and solace, and a sense of community, without favor. As he moved among the cots and long folding tables, he was fascinated to see how everyone, even the normally unruly downtown vagrant or two, became docile and quiet in what could be construed to be a church setting, with priests and nuns present. They were settling down peacefully. There was still respect for the cloth.

At the same time, his mind was halfway up the hill, worrying about Sandy Jones. A couple of things bothered him, even as he chatted amiably with the refugees. First was Anibel's wondering whether Jones could be trusted to turn himself in to the police in the morning. He could be, Hugh had assured her, but he knew the truth that Jones was too unhinged for assurances of any kind. The second was his conversation with Aloysius Logue, and the idea that big storms or other big events created their own narratives that were not in any way predictable. It was something he'd learned on the war's broad canvas, where no day could be known in advance, and no hour passed without a jack-in-the-box surprise. So it might be tonight. The image of Jones wouldn't leave him—up there in the big, empty house, desperately depressed and unhappy, erratic by nature. Would he dutifully march down to police headquarters in the morning? Would he lay out the full story for Detective Walker? Hugh suddenly realized that it was ridiculous to think so. Telling the nuns that he was going out to patrol local streets and look for those who might be in need, he got his Buick out of the garage and set out into the storm.

No one else was out driving, but it wasn't easy to get around. For the first time, Hugh saw the damage that the hurricane had already dealt out. A big tree across Prospect Street kept him from driving straight up to Jones' house. There didn't seem to be any power at all on the hill. The streetlights were out, and the houses were all in darkness, save for a few, like the Gills, with candlelight flickering from within. Hugh zigzagged his way among the fallen limbs and swirling leaves. At last he got to a spot where he could park and observe Jones' house. He turned off his headlights and then his engine. Now the darkness was complete. The rain continued to batter his windshield. All seemed quiet at the house—no lights, no candles. Hugh looked for any sort of movement at the windows but saw none. Jones' car stood in the driveway. That struck Hugh as odd. Why in the driveway and not in the nearby garage? He decided he'd wait a little longer, and then, after five minutes, he saw movement by the kitchen door—figures on the porch holding flashlights. The lights shook in their hands as they ran out to the car. One of the figures was notably larger than the other. Jones. It was he who got into the driver's side. For just a second, Jones' beam flashed across the face of his passenger—very young with long blond hair. The car's lights went on and it backed out of the driveway and proceeded past where Hugh was parked. He hid down low as it went by. Then he counted to 10, started up his car and set off, following at a safe distance. His dashboard clock read just a shade past midnight.

Again, almost no one was out on the streets, save for police cars, public works vehicles and Connecticut Light & Power trucks. Jones had a '49 Fleetwood coupe—possibly his last possession of any significance—and it was easy to follow its distinctive taillights, even from well back. He drove slowly. They went down North Main Street and past the eastern end of the Green, where the city's famous horse fountain needlessly splashed water into its overflowing trough. They were halfway down Bank Street, moving past the long block of retail stores, when all of

Waterbury's emergency sirens started up, filling the night with a screaming new level of urgency. Jones pulled over to the curb, as if wondering what the sirens meant and what he should do next. To Hugh, the sirens meant only one thing: something was happening with the river. Could it be that a dam, or several of them, had burst up north? He didn't know enough about the river system to be sure. But he felt certain that major trouble was on the way.

After a long moment, Jones set out again. Hugh followed, this time with his headlights out. As they crept along toward the Brooklyn section of town, Hugh realized they were headed right where they shouldn't be—the Bank Street Bridge, one of the city's handful of Naugatuck River crossings. As they approached the bridge, Hugh saw that someone had placed six or seven kerosene smudge pots across the roadway to keep motorists away. Their low, flickering flames were visible, barely, but they didn't create an effective barrier. Jones stopped his car again and got out. He began to kick the pots out of the way. Now Hugh got out of his car, too.

"Sandy, what are you doing!"

He had to shout against the roar of the water as it cascaded through one of the river's tightest corners. It felt like it was inches from running over its banks. Jones turned and said something unintelligible. Hugh moved closer to him and shouted the same question. Jones gestured toward his car.

"I have to get across!" Jones said. "I have to get someone home!"

"It isn't safe," Hugh said close to Jones' ear. "Even if you make it across, you won't make it back."

Things were now crashing loudly against the bridge—debris from upriver. Jones turned again to his car and waved. The passenger door swung open and the blond girl emerged and walked toward them. She seemed to be 12 or 13 years old.

"I wanted the experience one last time, Hugh," he said. "That's who I am now. I couldn't help myself."

The child came over and stood next to him. She was holding a silver candlestick.

"That's how I pay for things now. I use the family silver."

The noise of the rushing water was getting louder, drowning out even the sound of the sirens.

"Come with me," Jones said to Hugh, and the three of them went back to his car. He pulled something from the front seat, a familiar tube wrapped in brown paper.

"Here's the last one," he said. "Make sure it gets back to the Wheelers."

He then reached over and pulled the blonde wig from the child's head. The girl was a boy, terrified, pre-pubic, his brown hair cut short. Jones spoke to him.

"You go with Father Osgood and you will be safe," he said. "I can't do anything else about you now. Just go with him."

Jones turned to Hugh.

"He lives right over there, on the other side of the river, in the big tenement, with his poor mother, Ginny, who used to be a waitress at the club before she became an addict. If you can talk to her for me, I'd be grateful. On second thought, never mind. Maybe I'll do it myself."

With that, he got back into his car and closed the door. Hugh, for the boy's sake, thought it best to let Jones go. He stood back, his arm around the boy's shoulder, as the Cadillac crept off toward the bridge. He wanted to be the last to make it across safely, but instead he was the first not to. Just as he got to the middle of the span, the water swelled up yet again, this time over the railings, and slammed the car into the bridge wall. Jones was hurled out the windshield and up against the south rail, where he lingered a moment, frozen in his car's headlights, and then was swept away down into the watery night.

"We have to leave!" Hugh shouted to the boy.

They jumped into his car and sped away just as the bridge broke away entirely and the flood waters began to surge out across the city.

CHAPTER 14

Anibel drove down from Maine that Saturday, unaware of all that had happened in Waterbury during her brief absence. The flood had raged all night and through the next morning before beginning to relent. Up and down the valley, houses and apartments were swept away, factories wiped out, roads and rail lines uprooted. Scores of people were dead or missing. The water made it all the way from the riverbed up to the Waterbury Green, about a half-mile away, if not quite up the steps of the Immaculate or the rectory, or, for that matter, Anibel's own Mattatuck Museum, all of which had been built on slight rises. Electricity was out. Water was undrinkable. Helicopters flew over the scene, sometimes plucking people from rooftops. Sirens blared continually.

Anibel's drive south had taken her through other flooded areas of Connecticut, but the inconveniences had been minor. Coming in from the east, she didn't have to cross the Naugatuck. She could skirt the downtown on higher ground and get to her apartment, which was located well above flood level. She brought her suitcase in and sat down on her bed. Then she got up and went to her refrigerator to see what might spoil during the power blackout. She threw out some cream and a half-glass of tomato juice. Then she went back and sat on the bed again. She didn't know what to do. Maybe it *had* been a bad idea to come back. She needed to get in touch with her people at the museum, and she needed to get to Hugh. Again, she went over his revelations about Sandy Jones, the stolen paintings and the gold frames. Jones hadn't pulled the trigger on Dan, but he may as well have.

His perversions were behind everything. At length, Anibel realized that she could walk to the Gills' house. Their place, with all its moving parts, always seemed like a nerve center, and maybe it would be during the flood, too. Maybe Hugh would think the same thing.

◆ ◆ ◆

As to Hugh, he'd raced the flood and taken the boy straight back to the church. It seemed almost miraculous that there was a shelter with beds already set up there, and that he could, at least for the moment, leave him in the charge of whatever nuns were on duty. He'd learned that the boy was named Norman Henry, that he was 12, and that he lived with his mother and a younger sister in an apartment building he called Ward's Flats. Hugh told the nuns some of the boy's story, including the horror he'd just witnessed at the Bank Street bridge. He wanted them to know that shock was a possibility and that tender care was in order rather than their sterner classroom style. By the time Hugh left the shelter, the Green and its surrounds were flooded just enough so that he couldn't get to police headquarters in City Hall to let them know what had happened with Jones. He tried using the police call box located by the hotel next to the church, but that wasn't working, either. He'd have to wait. Somehow the truth of this entire colossal story now rested with him alone.

But he had more immediate life-and-death concerns to deal with. With only a vague word or two about where he'd been, and his narrow escape, Hugh joined the others at the rectory and the hastily drawn up plan put together by Monsignor Shutt. He'd had no sleep at all, but he'd join Father Ferraro for a predawn ride out to St. Mary's Hospital. Meanwhile, the other three priests would be arrayed between the shelter, the rectory (for rest) and the church itself, which would remain open, lit with dim emergency lights and candles for those who could get there. The priests would later rotate their positions. The Eucharist would of course continue to be celebrated.

Fortunately, Waterbury's two hospitals were located on opposite sides of the river, assuring the flood wouldn't cut anyone off from emergency care. The early morning scene at St. Mary's was extraordinarily busy, verging on chaotic. The battle footing Hugh had observed—could it only have been the day before?—was paying off as the ambulances came in, some having taken tortuous routes to stay on dry roads. Hugh walked along the line of gurneys in and around the Emergency Room, offering a word or two where he could. Several of the faces were covered with sheets. For them, Hugh lifted the covering and said Last Rites. Catholic or not, he always thought, the ritual would do no harm.

Around noon, he was standing by the Emergency Room entrance when he noticed that one of the flood victims was being delivered not by an ambulance, but rather by a police vehicle, a kind of a cross between a Jeep and a paddy wagon. He asked the cops if they were returning to headquarters anytime soon, which they were, and within 15 minutes, after plowing through two feet of water, he found himself at the desk sergeant's high counter, asking for Detective Walker, saying he had a story to tell.

A couple of hours later, Hugh felt emptied and cleansed, as if he'd been to confession himself. He'd told the entire story as he knew it. Detail after detail had come rolling out to Walker, who barely had to open his mouth. At length, the true order of events —Sandy Jones, Creasy, Valuckas, Murphy—had been restored. Justice had been or would assuredly be visited upon those responsible. When he was done, Hugh walked away from City Hall toward the Green. Already the flood had receded enough so that he could trudge through about 6 inches of water back to the rectory. He rolled up his trouser legs and carried his shoes and socks. Once on the other side, he sat on the church steps, methodically put his shoes and socks back on, rolled down his trouser legs, and then, instead of entering the rectory, continued his walk up the hill, past the fallen tree that had blocked his way the night before, all the way up to the Gill's house, where he felt a full recounting deserved to be heard. When he came through the back door and saw Anibel there, standing in the kitchen, talking quietly with Mrs. Gill, he sat down, put his head in his hands and at last allowed his emotions to cascade out in great, sobbing waves.

Anibel was the first to go. She always was good at seeing the big picture, and after a couple of months had gone by, she thought it possible that the flood had dealt Waterbury such a devastating blow that it might never recover, and that the steady decline in the brass mills and other manufacturers would only be hastened. Whether she was wrong or right about that, she didn't like her own prospects if she stayed around. Her associations with the city—every street, park, building and lamppost—had grown largely negative. Beyond negative, actually. Dan had turned into a ghost, ready to spring out or slowly materialize at any time, in any place. For Anibel, his presence proved over and over again that there doesn't have to be only one love in life; there can be two or even more. She also knew that her only path forward was to get away from both of hers. She looked at many job openings before settling on the Stanford University Museum of Art, in California, which needed help getting back on its feet following many years of neglect. She wouldn't be director, but she'd have a significant position, proximity to intellectual and cultural treasures, and what she hoped would be the steadying presence of the vast blue Pacific.

She'd made Hugh aware of her desire to leave, and he didn't dare try to stand in her way. When the time finally came, in the spring of 1956, he offered to drive her to New York's Idlewild Airport for her flight west, but she'd said no.

"Forgive me, Hugh, but I don't want a lingering, wistful goodbye that's subject to traffic conditions. I'm still not in the mood for that."

They were seated in bright sunshine on a bench near the pedestal clock at the center of the Waterbury Green. Around the clock's base, a circle of tulips was bursting with red. This would be Anibel and Hugh's last conversation for a very long time.

"I envy you the plane ride," said Hugh. "The idea that people can just pack up and leave is amazing to me."

"You can do it, too. You're in the perfect profession for it. You can always go to Rome, can't you?

Hugh wondered how he'd ever manage without Anibel as a continuing presence in his life.

"Maybe," he said, "but I do have Norman to worry about. I feel like I owe him something."

"I'd say it's the opposite," Anibel said. "You saved him, you shielded him as best you could from the drowning of his mother and sister, and you made sure he found a good home with a solid family. How much more are you expected to do?"

"I know."

"He's on his own now, in a way."

"I know."

Anibel stood. She was ready to go.

"It's been a terrible year, Hugh," she said with a teary smile. "I'll miss you."

"I'll miss you, too. Maybe you should stay."

"No. As long as you can think of me every day and be miserable, even if just for that brief moment, I'll be happy."

"You'll be very happy then."

They embraced. Anibel kissed Hugh's cheek affectionately, and then his forehead. Then she walked across the street, back up the hill, and away.

◆ ◆ ◆

Hugh's leave-taking was less complicated. He didn't have anyone to say goodbye to—not anyone like Anibel. He stayed around long enough to bear witness on Dan's behalf to the life-in-prison sentencing of Robert Creasy. He decided that Anibel had been right about Norman Henry. The boy didn't need the steady presence of a priest in his life, he needed a shot at normalcy and family affection. With a break here or there, it wouldn't be too late for him.

It was time for Hugh to fly, too. Given all the many extenuating circumstances, the Church hierarchy had been lenient with him. With the understanding that he might wish to leave the Immaculate, he was remarkably free to choose his own course. As he thought about his next move, he returned again and again to Old Joe Mulry's crusade for social justice in the Philippines. That's what Hugh wanted to do, too. Deep down, he always had. But it wasn't the Philippines that he was thinking of. In 1956, it was impossible to be unaware of the struggles and unrest taking place in America's Deep South—the bus boycott in Montgomery, the resistance to the court-ordered integration of schools, the beatings and murders of those peacefully seeking their basic civil rights. Hugh couldn't miss the important roles the northern clergy were beginning to play in it, either. He hadn't read about too many Catholic priests early on, but maybe it was time for them to join in, too. As for him, he'd jumped into worse spots in his life, also for a worthy cause, and found he could do some good. That was the feeling he wanted to get back again, both the jumping and the feeling good.

So, one late afternoon in the fall, with his parents, Dan Gill and Anibel, in fact all his loved ones here and gone, urging him on from behind like a favoring breeze, he lifted his bag onto a Trailways bus headed for Washington, Richmond and points south. Was it too much for him to wish that God would yet again be with him and keep him safe? Maybe this one last time, he thought. He settled into his seat, said a silent, final farewell to Waterbury, and, just to be on the safe side, touched his collar three times for luck as the bus roared out of town.

ACKNOWLEDGEMENTS

I was a five-year-old Waterburian during the spring and summer of 1955, when this story is set, so I can't claim to know many of that year's events and details purely by memory. I do vividly recall '55's great August flood, especially, as a child would, its hovering rescue helicopters and the sound of the Naugatuck River as it roared down the valley. My more sustained Waterbury memories don't kick in until about 1960, but I guess they can serve 1955 well enough. Older or more observant local souls might find a detail or two out of place, but, in general, when it comes to Waterbury, I'm going with what I know.

Other aspects of the book did require outside sources, however, even beyond what Wikipedia could provide. My depiction of the Los Banos prison camp in the Philippines and the profile of Rev. Joseph Mulry owes much to "The Gentle Warrior: The Story of Fr. George J. Willmann, S.J." by James B. Reuter, S.J. and "Experiences in the Philippines in World War II" by Mulry's contemporary W. C. Repetti, S.J. Similarly, a portion of the account of Dan Gill's time with *Stars and Stripes* in North Africa and Italy draws directly from the wartime memories of Herbert Mitgang, published in the April 1971 issue of *American Heritage*. The story of the Wheelers' adventures in 19th-Century Impressionism owes much to *Hidden in Plain Sight: The Whittemore Collection and the French Impressionists* by Ann Y. Smith.

On a personal note, I am grateful for the support of early readers of the manuscript, including Tom "Pro" Riley, my dear mother

Rosemary Brady Monagan, brother Michael, children John, Matt and Claire, and, of course, their mother, Marcia, who kept me on task and went to the whip hand only rarely.

ABOUT THE AUTHOR

Charles Monagan

Charles Monagan has been a writer and editor since 1972, when he graduated from Dartmouth College. His work has appeared in many magazines and newspapers, and from 1989 to 2013 he was the Editor of Connecticut Magazine. In 1997, he won the Gold Medal for Reporting from the national City and Regional Magazine Association. In 2012, he received the Connecticut Press Club's Mark Twain Award for Distinguished Journalism, a lifetime award.

Monagan is the author of 10 books, including The Neurotic's Handbook, The Reluctant Naturalist, How to Get a Monkey into Harvard and the novel Carrie Welton. Additionally, he wrote the book and lyrics for the music Mad Bomber, which was produced in 2011 and won first place in the Academy for New Musical Theatre's 2012 international Search for New Musicals.

Monagan and his wife, Marcia, live in Connecticut.

Made in the USA
Coppell, TX
08 November 2020